Eclectically
Magical

Eclectic Writings Series

Eclectically Magical

Eclectic Series Vol. 6

Compiled by

Fern Brady and Kelly Colby

Inklings Publishing

www.inklingspublishing.com

Compiled by Fern Brady, Kelly Colby, and Karina Winbigler

Copyedited/Formatted by D Tinker Editing

Cover Art by Verstandt

ISBN: 978-1-944428-97-6 by Inklings Publishing
http://inklingspublishing.com

First US Edition

Printed in the United States of America

22 21 20 19 18   1 2 3 4 5

To all authors.

Thank you for keeping the dream alive

and bringing the magic of words

to the world.

Table of Contents

Acknowledgments

Inklings Publishing is proud to bring readers great stories by amazing authors, both new and established, through our anthologies. The Inklings team wishes to thank all the authors who have entrusted their work to us so that we may put it in the hands of as many fans as possible. We look forward to producing many more volumes in the years to come.

Fern Brady would like to thank the whole Inklings team for their support of the company and the beautiful work they do. She sends a special thanks to her husband and Inklings president, Mike Brady, for being on this journey with her. As always, she sends love and kisses to the Inklings mascots: her two dogs, Merlin and Arya. Most especially, she continues to give thanks to the Great I Am, whose grace and favor continuously amaze her and without whom she would be nothing at all.

Kelly Colby would like to thank Fern Brady, CEO of Inklings Publishing, for trusting her enough to work with these authors to make this anthology amazing. Everyone needs someone in their life who helps them get to the next level. Fern is doing that for Kelly, and she is grateful. Kelly also has to thank her husband for always being supportive, regardless of how many hours she locks herself away in her office or at a coffee shop. Kevin Colby keeps her sane with encouragement. She couldn't do it without him. Lastly, Kelly wants to thank the readers. Those of you who explore fantastical worlds, gifted magicians, and enchanted heroes are the reason we all keep writing.

We hope you enjoy the journey as much as we've enjoyed creating it.

Sneezes

Ashley Lynn Field

"But where shall I go?"

"I'm sure the next town over will take you, my dear."

Ana frowned at the rotund man who blocked the tall gates into the village where she had been born and raised.

"Due to an unfortunate incident involving Madam Wharton's rear end sprouting roses, I'm afraid they won't have me, either. Madam was quite angry with me," Ana muttered, glancing sideways.

"My dear," the portly mayor repeated. "You must know this pains me greatly. You are such a kindhearted girl, but the village has spoken and I must comply."

"This isn't because of the issue with your wife, is it, John?" Ana tucked a rogue strand of hair behind her ear.

John glanced quickly behind him, where a beady-eyed woman glared out of the gatehouse window.

"Come now, Ana, we agreed not to speak of that. Poor Meredith wouldn't come out of the house for weeks."

"I know her warts began to sing, but they eventually left to go on tour. I did what I promised and rid her of her ailment. I'm not sure why she's so put out with the whole thing."

John patted her shoulder cautiously. "Ana, they named themselves Warts and Roses, and they play at the inn every Friday."

Ana muffled a sigh and crossed her arms. "A few mishaps should not wipe out years of service as the town healer!"

"Two weeks ago, you had the school children burping up frogs."

"It was an excellent teaching exercise that they found hilarious!"

"And last week, you managed to make it snow for four days, effectively wiping out a whole crop of carrots."

"It was so hot that day," she practically whined. "You know I can't control what happens."

"And just today, you were responsible for turning half of Abigail's livestock from goats into cats! What is that poor woman going to do with thirty cats?"

"Die alone?" Ana whispered under her breath before adding, "What you're neglecting to see is that I solved our mice problem."

"Sort your craft out and you will be more than welcome to return, but until then . . ."

"Until then, you will not have me?"

The man nodded, his double chin flapping in agreement. "We cannot survive you, I'm afraid," he said, backing away from Ana.

She sniffed, lifting a hand to pinch her nostrils together. Her dapple-gray gelding, Igloo, stood ten paces away, placidly munching hay and flicking his ears to get rid of a fly.

"Ana," warned John. A bead of sweat threatened to drip down his round face.

"It's just the hay. I should be fine," she said with an uncertain smile.

"Have a nice life!" he shouted and ran faster than Ana had ever imagined he could, given his generous size. Slamming the village gate behind him, she heard him shout, "Flee for your lives!"

"Rude," Ana hissed just before a sneeze erupted from her nose, causing the previously sturdy village gate to transform into ten or so monkeys.

The animals, momentarily stunned by their creation, soon began leaping happily about, tipping over carts of fruit, stealing hats from the heads of both men and women, and eventually absconding with Ana's sack.

"Well, that's just lovely," Ana said, wide-eyed. Whatever chance she stood of being allowed back into her village had just vanished along with her belongings.

Ana and Igloo plodded slowly along the Great Road, enjoying the mix of magic and innovation used to create it.

Several years ago, after the death of the queen, the king, in his grief, delved into revamping the country's infrastructure. He began by widening the Great Road, filling deep potholes, and digging trenches in areas likely to flood.

Lost in thoughts of hat-stealing monkeys, it took Ana a few hours to realize she was being followed.

She wasn't sure why she hadn't noticed before, as the man was doing an abysmal job of hiding. He would toss himself bodily into the bushes at random intervals—leaving his horse still standing on the road. Occasionally, he would veer his steed in a circle and head the opposite direction when he saw Ana looking. Her favorite ruse involved him shouting "Fox!" before directing his horse into the underbrush, as if he belonged to a hunting party.

Ana waited for the man to return from one such foray before meeting him head-on.

"Hello," she said, making eye contact and smiling, half-afraid he would dart off after another imaginary fox. "I'm Ana."

"Oh. Well. Yes. I know that, I guess."

"You've been following me."

The man nodded sheepishly. "I was afraid you would sneeze. Still am, if we're being honest." He scratched the three hairs on his chin he considered a beard.

Ana rolled her eyes. A few little magical mishaps brought on by hay fever and the whole world becomes afraid of you.

"Well, on with it, then. The dust might kick up at any moment," Ana quipped.

The man shrank back, his eyes going wide.

"I don't do it on purpose!" she reprimanded, causing both horses to shy sideways.

A gifted healer since childhood, Ana had woken up one day to find herself performing wild acts of magic upon sneezing—something her patients began to fear after Ana managed to turn Tanya May's toes into tiny worms.

She had fixed the offending feet, of course, but Tanya May wouldn't talk to Ana for a week. Which was ridiculous, really. And after Ana had cured her fungus.

"I don't suppose you have a name?" Ana asked archly.

"It's Billy, miss. You turned my cousin's house into a waterfall once," commented the man with the unsuccessful beard. Ana wanted to recommend a salve for hair growth but thought this wasn't the time, perhaps.

"Well, that isn't too bad!" she said. "Who wouldn't want a nice water feature in their home?"

"She can't swim."

Ana waved an unconcerned hand in the air. "Obviously she will learn. I've done her a favor; drownings are so common."

"Oh, she almost did."

Ana's eyes widened in horror. She vaguely recalled turning a group of floundering women into flounder, which she had considered poetic at the time.

"You saved her, though, which was nice. It's why I'm here."

"To thank me?" asked Ana.

"I guess not," he started. "I figure it was your fault she was around the water to begin with."

"Well, that's . . . logical."

"Anyway, I thought, as you did save her and all, that I would tell you what I know about your . . . your . . ."

"Condition," finished Ana.

"Yes. That. It's a curse."

"What?" she shouted, startling the horses. "Why would anyone want to curse me? Well, before I started turning gates into monkeys, of course."

"It was a hag from the Netherwood, but that's all I know," he said, his chin hairs twitching in regret.

"The Netherwood?"

The man nodded. "It's the half-burnt forest west of the castle. Home to a lot of shady folk, apparently. Something about the aesthetic."

"That sounds slightly unappealing," Ana mumbled.

He shrugged. "I've heard the check-in clerk keeps a list of clients, so if you give them your name, you should be able to see which hag put the curse on you."

"How very businesslike," Ana said, her mind already drifting to being welcomed back into her village.

"If you don't mind, miss, I don't want my family to find out I told you. They are still a bit miffed over the whole kitchen-turning-into-a-pond thing. The kids were trout for a few days, which they enjoyed, but their momma was in a fit state. She almost cooked the youngest."

"I can see how that would be . . . well, yes, thank you." She sniffed and felt a tiny tickle in her left nostril. "I think I might sneeze," she squeaked in warning.

Her stalker reigned his horse to the left and dug in his heels, shouting "Good luck!" as he galloped away.

Ana rubbed her nose and felt the tickle worsen. "Maybe I'll get my bag back," she said aloud, thinking fondly of her favorite hairbrush while she ran her fingers through her quickly tangling hair.

She supposed it was a good thing there was no one around to talk to.

As Ana thought this, a sneeze tore through her, and she carefully blinked her eyes back open. Surely she couldn't do much harm as there was no one and nothing really around. Just the road, some dust, and— well, that was interesting. Did the trees always have faces like that? They might have; she had been distracted by her follower earlier.

"'Scuse me, miss," said one tree to her right. "You wouldn't happen to know if we've always had the ability to talk, would you? Not sure I rightly recall, meself."

Ana compressed her lips into a thin line and glanced heavenward. "I believe that skill is newly acquired. That would be my fault, I'm afraid."

"It's all right!" cried another tree. "I quite like having a face. It's easier to threaten the squirrels this way. My nose itches a bit, though. It's all the dust. Don't reckon you could scratch it for me, eh?"

Ana obliged, spending the better part of an hour scratching noses.

She couldn't have known that she'd created a forest that would be considered haunted in years to come. All the dust kicked up by passersby would rankle the poor trees into itching fits, turning their moods sour and causing them to scream at anyone passing along their section of road.

Ana traveled along a narrow offshoot of the Great Road looking for the Netherwood, which was remarkably well advertised. Signs as far back as a week's journey pointed the way, promising cheap curses, unbreakable love potions, and painless enlargements of all kinds.

During the trip, she helped one lady with a bone spur, rescued an inquisitive cat from a swarm of angry bees, and turned an apple orchard into a field of marshmallow fluff.

She chalked the last one up as a win because the townsfolk were incredibly happy with this turn of events. Their apples had been up against too much competition from other orchards, but now the village had the market cornered with the sugary confection.

Upon finally reaching the Netherwood, Ana was mostly let down. She had been expecting something dark, foreboding, and maybe a bit scary, but the front of the forest was lit up like a village square during a double-wedding ceremony.

Ana's eyes were accosted by magically blinking signs, arrows pointing to different paths, and—the tackiest of all—a woman dressed as a fairy standing in front of a hollowed-out log. A sign that read *Concierge* twinkled just to the right of the fairy wannabe.

Ana had never met a fairy, but she had studied them in school.

They were very helpful little critters, when they weren't being total pests. They replenished worm populations, removed rocks from gardens, and even righted fallen bird feeders, but that was only if they liked you.

If they didn't care for you, they would turn all your desserts into prunes.

"'Ello," muttered the human-sized fake fairy.

"Uh, yes. I'm looking for the hag who cursed me," Ana stated as she flung a leg over Igloo's back. The gelding tossed a questioning look at his master before meandering off to nip at the tall grass bordering the woods. "It's some sort of sneezing curse. Every time I sneeze, something ridiculous happens," Ana added.

The dark-haired woman frowned. "Name?"

"Ana."

"Well, it needs to be your full name, doesn't it?"

"Victoriana Oatbringer. My family used to raise oats."

The concierge nodded as if this were all incredibly boring. She blew a fluffy curl of black hair out of her face before flipping open a bulky leather-bound tome sitting atop her makeshift podium.

She mumbled in annoyance as she paged through the yellowed vellum, tossing glances at Ana, who didn't notice.

The air behind the faux fairy wavered, causing it to turn blue and then purple, as if something was shifting behind her. Ana found it vastly distracting.

"What kind of enchantment is that?" asked Ana. "It's very pretty. I've never seen one that does anything like that."

The green-eyed woman perked up and tilted her head. "You can see that?"

"Well, the air behind you looks a bit like a melting rainbow."

"Dancing pigs, you *can* see them!"

"I'm not perfectly sure what I'm seeing, but I do see something," offered Ana, realizing the unhelpful nature of her admission.

"Those are my wings! No one has been able to see them in *ages!*"

"You're an actual fairy, then?" Ana asked, disbelief written across her face.

"'Course I'm a fairy. Name's Penelope. The Norwhich Nether Hag, Rutle, bound me to service, or I wouldn't be here."

"That's very rude of her," Ana said sensibly.

Penelope nodded, her mop of curly hair bobbing. "I'm mostly certain she was the one who cursed you, since you can see my wings. Not sure why you aren't on the master list, though."

"Can you take me to her?"

"My pleasure! Although I doubt it will do much good. Rutle is a soulless wench who only takes enjoyment in the misery of others."

Ana moaned. "She sounds lovely."

Penelope led Ana through the maze of the Netherwood to a massive brightly glowing green toadstool. The front door was enchanted to look like a pulsating spider web.

"This is all very—"

"Tasteless?" Penelope finished.

Ana nodded.

"The Netherwood was once rather spooky," stated the fairy. "Half of it was burned down when the prince—rest his soul—tried to set up camp but left his fire unattended. He was lost in the fire, poor dear, and the combination of death and destruction drew a goodly number of hags to the area. A few of the saggy crones began losing business because they were farther back into the woods than their sisters, so the nasty sacks of bones added a slew of glaring signs to guide people to them. After a handful of years, it became this abuse to the eyes."

Penelope kicked open the front door of the garish shop. "Rutle, you got a customer!" the fairy barked unhappily.

A barrage of smells clamored to be the first up Ana's nose. Sour and dusty, sweet and peppery, musty and green all slammed into her face, causing her eyes to water. She tried desperately not to sneeze. She didn't want to shrink the hag's home as an introduction.

"You get used to it," Penelope said with a shrug. "Or your nose melts off your face and you can never smell anything ever again. Either way."

A hunched crone of a woman with enough warts, wrinkles, and

ear hair to create a new person stirred a large neon-green cauldron in the back of the room.

"She's making lunch," Penelope whispered loudly. "The old bag wants people to think she brews potions in that thing, but it's just food."

"Should have used you for parts," Rutle grumbled at Penelope.

Ana fought a snicker and a sneeze and then loudly pronounced, "It seems as if you've cursed me."

"Were you in the book?" creaked the wrinkle pile.

"Well, no—"

"Then I didn't curse you."

"It's definitely your magic," countered Penelope, earning a withering glare. "She can see me wings."

The hag sighed. "Name?"

"Victoriana—"

"Haven't used any magic on a Victoriana."

"I go by Ana most of the time."

The hag threw a pinch of salt into her cauldron and perked up. "Now, I *have* cursed several Anas."

The frizzy-haired crone pulled out a covered binder and threw it on a badly scarred wooden table in front of Ana. She leafed through the pages, squinting.

"Carrot juice every morning is good for eyesight," Ana stated before she could stop herself.

The hag looked up from her folder and mumbled something about insufferable healers.

"There you are," she said finally, after Ana was sure the heap of skin had fallen asleep.

Ana picked up a sheaf of yellowed paper and read, "Ana the Oathbreaker? That isn't me. Obviously."

The crone frowned, her wrinkles struggling to crease further. "What?"

"My name is Victoriana Oatbringer . . . because my family used to grow oats."

Shrugging, the hag swiped the paper from Ana and shoved it back into place inside the binder. "A curse was paid for and a curse was delivered."

"But you delivered it to the wrong person!"

"Doesn't matter. Read the fine print."

"I didn't sign anything, you loony bat!" cried Ana, her brows creasing in annoyance. Every miserable mishap of the last two years was due to the bad eyesight of a Netherwood hag?

"Already paid for," the hag insisted again.

"Then I'll pay you to reverse it," Ana snarked back.

"Don't be daft. If word got out that a Hag of the Nether was taking coin to reverse her curses—"

"You would be twice as rich," finished Ana dryly.

"No one would use a hag that could be paid off. It goes against our code of ethics," tutted Rutle, as if shocked everyone did not already know this.

"I've met people petty enough to consider a temporary curse a good lesson. There was this one town of people that didn't like me because I—"

"Don't care," Rutle muttered, ambling back to her simmering pot.

"I will camp on your doorstep if you don't cure me of this!"

"A wailing girl on my front stoop would do me wonders," Rutle responded, unperturbed. "Actually, would you be interested in signing a contract with me?"

Ana stared, wide-eyed, at the foul creature.

"You're *horrible*," she whispered, distraught.

Penelope shifted to Ana's right, obviously uncomfortable with the exchange. She caught the healer's eye and motioned to a dark urn full of softly glowing yellow powder.

Curious, Ana leaned in closer to read the label and immediately sneezed three times.

Penelope was turned into a frog, the cooking pot into a large rock (with a pretty sort of green moss growing on the side), and a thunderstorm clapped into existence outside.

Rutle sighed, glancing longingly at the rock that had previously been the makings of a decidedly delicious dinner.

Ana squeaked in horror before snatching Penelope up. "I'm so sorry!" she cooed at the frog.

Croaking twice, the frog puffed itself out into a purple bubble and popped, leaving behind a rainbow puff of smoke.

"Well, that was interesting," Ana commented with a shrug. She'd never turned a fairy into a frog before.

"You cost me my fairy, you rotten girl!" screeched Rutle. "Do you know how much business she brought in?"

"Where did she go?" Ana asked, her eyes squinting in confusion.

"She's no longer a fairy while she's a frog, is she? My curses only last as long as people are what they are."

"So, if I could turn myself into a toad—"

"But you can't, now can you? Everything you do affects those around you, but never yourself. What you *can* do is replace my front desk staff."

Ana arched a brow in defiance.

Rutle clarified. "I need something that will draw business in. You don't think I can lure people in on my own, do you?"

"I don't know how you stand on your own," Ana muttered. Louder, she added, "You expect me to entrap another creature against their will?"

"No, you brat. I expect you to replace what you have lost me. I would use you, but humans are lousy marketers. Especially whiny ones with allergies."

Ana shook her head. "Nope. Not going to help you."

Frustratingly tranquil, Rutle sniffed and hobbled off to the back of her large toadstool. A few minutes later, she came out of a back room carrying a cage covered in a black cloth. Its inhabitant made loud cawing noises.

"This is Hank," Rutle said, pulling a large inky-black crow from the cage. "Hank will accompany you and make sure you don't get into any trouble."

"But I said—"

"Do you know what a hex is, little girl? Go out and fetch my replacement, or I will drain your life from you in a matter of hours."

Ana's eyes widened in abject horror. Wasn't a curse bad enough?

"Get out of my shop!"

With that, Rutle cast Ana out of the Netherwood and left her standing at the entrance. Hank hopped around at her feet.

He looked up at her dolefully and shrugged as best a crow could. "I would say you get used to her, but you don't. She's just awful, honestly. She makes boiled cabbage at least three times a week."

"Oh, good, you talk."

"Of course I talk. You talk. Why wouldn't I talk?"

Ana pressed her lips together and sighed through her nose, which caused one last sneeze.

Hank was now a wallaby.

He rocked back onto his tail and kicked his feet. "This is new. I like it. Can I stay this way?"

"Well, aren't you free now?" she asked, baffled.

Hank shook his adorably fuzzy head. "I'm not cursed. I signed a voluntary agreement as a familiar."

"Why would you do that?"

"Lots of reasons. Mine was in exchange for something."

"For what?" Ana asked as she scooped the adorable ball of fluff up into her arms.

Hank nuzzled down against her and made himself comfortable while Ana settled herself on her patient gelding.

"Oh, I'm not sure I recall now; it's been a while," he stated, sticking his tongue out to test its length. "I might miss flying, though," he mumbled. Hank kicked his feet two more times before totally settling down.

"How long is the contract for?" she asked, appalled.

"Most familiars sign on for life. Not on purpose, mind you."

Ana puffed out her cheeks. That seemed awfully unfair, didn't it? To sign one's life away and not even recall what it was for.

"Are you . . . I mean, were you . . . human?" Ana felt vaguely embarrassed about the question but wasn't entirely sure why.

Flicking his long ears, Hank tilted his head to the side. "Possibly," he answered truthfully.

Ana patted Igloo's neck and directed the horse back to the road.

"Oh, you need to head south. To the Burning Peaks," Hank added with a yawn.

"Why would I do that?" Ana inquired.

"Rutle wants a replacement—a dragon egg—and that is where we need to go to acquire one."

"She wants me to steal a dragon's egg?" Ana asked, feeling an ache building between her temples.

"Well, not steal," Hank amended. "The dragons of the Burning Peaks occasionally donate an egg to Rutle to keep her from plundering the nurseries far more often. I believe she intends to raise this one instead of using the shell for her love spells."

"That's how you make a love spell?" Ana asked, repulsed. "The thought of that bag of bones raising a dragon is almost as bad, though."

Hank yawned again. "I don't imagine you have much of a choice. A hex from Rutle is a death sentence."

"I was hoping she was joking," groused Ana with a slump of her shoulders.

The Burning Peaks were at the very southern border of the king's land, much farther than Ana had ever been. Most of the mountains were active volcanoes, which occasionally spit fiery spews of molten rock down onto the foothills.

Signs that read *Death from Above* littered the surrounding area. A few were on fire.

Igloo huffed in annoyance when Ana drew him up short before a massive stone gate that arched above them.

Hank (currently a bright-white mongoose via one of Ana's sneezes) craned his neck to stare up.

"This is lovely," Ana commented, gesturing to the tremendous set of carved stone jaws gaping in welcome. Runes etched along the side begged caution of anyone passing this point.

"It's bigger than I remember," muttered Hank.

"You've been here before?"

The mongoose nodded. "Not sure why, though."

"Death wish, I assume," Ana quipped, eyeing a smoking cluster of trees. "These dragons are going to let us traipse right in and abscond with one of their eggs, eh? Granted, I suppose it would solve both of our issues if I were roasted alive," she said dryly.

"Are you that unhappy?" Hank asked, concerned. "You don't seem unhappy."

"I don't suppose I am," she said after a moment's thought. "I think I was for a while, but I seem to be much better now."

Hank scratched his small fuzzy jaw with his back foot before adding, "You're welcome."

"You're not *that* charming," she protested. "Knowing who and what caused my condition helped."

A tiny meteor of fire whistled down beside the trio, spooking Igloo. The dust-covered gelding danced sideways in fright, almost unseating Ana.

"I don't think it would be wise to take him past the gate," Hank said. "I'm sure he could do with a repose, anyway."

Nodding in agreement, Ana kicked her leg over the saddle and leaped to the rocky, uneven ground. "I won't be long," she promised her long-suffering horse. "And if I am," she added, "I'm probably dead. In which case, you likely should return home."

Igloo, showing no signs of feeling rejected, wandered off toward a copse of long grass that had not been burned to cinders, while Ana and Hank made their way through the stone archway.

As the day grew longer, the duo began to wilt. Sweat poured down Ana's brow, stinging her eyes and soaking her hair. Hank looked as if he would pass out at any moment, his fluffy white pelt trapping the heat against his skin.

"I don't think being a mongoose is very wise while climbing a volcano," he commented glumly.

"I don't think being anything on a volcano is very wise," added Ana. "You look ill," she said, picking him up.

"I don't suppose you could fix it?" he asked pitifully.

Undauntedly cheerful for the majority of the last several weeks, Hank had never once complained. For him to ask something of her now, Ana realized he must be truly suffering.

The thought made her heart hurt.

He had been so supportive and kind to her, a constant bolster to her mood. She wanted to be able to offer him something in return.

"I will try," she promised. "Maybe I can make it snow?"

"Just turn me into something better suited," he said with simple confidence.

"You know I can't control it, Hank," Ana said in defeat.

Hank wiggled against her, trying to find comfort. "What do you think of when you sneeze?"

"Oh?" What did she think about? Mostly that she shouldn't sneeze, she guessed.

"Perhaps your thoughts have an effect on what happens after?"

Ana puffed out her cheeks in thought. Maybe Hank was onto something? When Tanya May was wiggling her fungus-riddled toes in her face, Ana had thought they looked a bit like worms, and then they became worms (fungus-free worms, at that). And when riding through the apple orchard weeks ago, Ana had thought she wanted to eat something sweeter than an apple . . . a marshmallow, in particular.

"By the saints," she whispered.

Kissing Hank's nose, she sat him down and reached for a singed blade of grass.

"I think you're a genius!" She shoved the grass into her nose, causing a sneeze. (Nothing is itchier than burnt grass.)

Before Hank could digest the dichotomy of her words versus her actions, he had been transformed into a large green iguana.

"I've been so busy trying not to sneeze that I never once concentrated on what was going through my head when I *did*!" Happy tears welled against her lashes, threatening to spill over the delicate barrier. "No one has ever tried to help me. Mostly because they were terrified, mind you."

If she could control this curse, then it wouldn't be so much of a curse as a boost to her abilities. She would have to be careful regarding random sneezes, but for the most part, she could focus on something benign when she felt the tickle of a sneeze coming on.

"You're welcome, Ana," Hank said, a curious expression on his scaly face.

"We are leaving," Ana commanded, a smile on her lips. "We will simply travel about until we find a town suitable enough for both of us. Rutle will forget about us eventually." She winked.

"She has your name, Ana," Hank said sadly. "If we do not return, she can hex you from her toadstool."

"I'm surprised the saggy battle-axe hasn't already," Ana muttered. "Well, when we get back, we're going to look over your contract. I have a feeling you've already served it out. And even if you haven't," she added, "someone like you shouldn't be around a vile thing like Rutle."

"If we return without an egg, she'll definitely hex you," Hank commented, his voice quaking angrily.

"Is there any situation in which I do not get hexed?" Ana asked crossly.

"I would apologize for eavesdropping, but allowing for how loud you two are, I cannot imagine you are trying to hide your conversation," interrupted a voice from behind the duo.

Ana spun around to chastise whomever had spoken (it was incredibly rude to eavesdrop and then interrupt to boot!) and fell flat on her rear upon seeing a large golden dragon peering down at her.

"I—we—Rutle—" stammered Ana.

The dragon fanned her elephantine ears in amusement. "I heard. Most of the mountain heard, actually." The great beast turned her head slightly, scales glinting in the last rays of the sun before it tipped behind the range of volcanoes. "I am Elidin, since it doesn't seem likely anyone will ask me."

"Haven't we met before?" asked Hank, the memory a tickle against his mind.

"I see I am as unforgettable as ever," Elidin preened. "We have met, yes, but there is a nasty rumor floating around that you're dead."

The little lizard puffed out his neck flap. "I suppose I got better."

"You recognize him like this?" asked Ana, curious.

"Contracts are base magic," the dragon said with a hiss. "They cast a shadow over the creature affected, but we dragons can see through it." Elidin sniffed. "I'm not insinuating that dragons are better than everyone else, of course."

"So you can see what he is?" pressed Ana.

"Human. He wouldn't talk so much if he were anything else."

Ana glanced down at Hank and fought a smile.

"There is a way to stop Rutle from pillaging our eggs and keep the two of you safe as well," commented Elidin.

"Yes! How?" exclaimed Ana, grabbing Hank and jumping to her feet. Not dying would be an excellent way to end her adventure.

"As I said before, contracts are a base magic and therefore susceptible to fire. Hags fireproof their dwellings to avoid this, but dragon fire is magical—much better than normal fire." Elidin flicked her tongue.

"Why haven't you burned the contracts before?" asked Ana before she could school her thoughts.

"We cannot get access to the Netherwood. The hags came together and warded the woods against us. If we get near it, we itch."

Ana's brow raised a notch. "You . . ."

"Itch, yes," finished Elidin.

"How do we get you past the wards?" questioned Hank.

"I cannot pass through the wards physically, but I can be summoned from *inside* of the wards without any itchy side effects."

"I've never summoned anything before," Ana said hesitantly.

"I wouldn't expect you to be able to," Elidin said. "I will give you a summoning pearl for that singular purpose. You two must go back to the Netherwood and use it. I will handle the fiery part."

The next morning, much to Igloo's abject horror, Elidin flew the three of them to a village that had recently become well-known for their fields of marshmallow fluff.

"Rest here until dark," commanded the golden beast as she carefully handed Ana a large pearl. "At dusk, head for the Netherwood and use this to call me. I will be ready."

Ana thanked Elidin profusely, her heart light with the thought of Hank being freed.

"This will not be a cure for your curse," warned the dragon. "Only those affected by contracts will be freed."

"Will Ana be safe from being hexed?" Hank asked with audible concern for his friend.

"In my infinite wisdom, I have arranged for a representative of the king to be at the Netherwood." Here, Elidin made a show of winking at Hank. "All hags will be transported via fairy to the castle and held under ward. They will not be able to access their supplies or their magic. There will be no hexing on my watch, to be sure."

"My dear, our village has never done so well since you changed our fields to fluff! I owe you a debt. We all do!" declared the mayor. "Anything you need is yours." The mayor beamed and patted Ana on the back in a fatherly manner.

"Just a bath and a warm meal," she answered, realizing she smelled of sulfur.

Slipping down into the hot water of her metal tub, Ana checked again that the paper folding screen was hiding her from Hank. It was silly to hide from an iguana, but Hank was human, after all.

"You will miss me," Hank teased playfully.

"I will not," Ana insisted, relaxing down into the water further.

"Rude," hissed Hank.

"Where will you go once you become human again?" Ana asked.

"I was hoping to stay with you. But that was before you were rude."

Ana laughed. "I would be very put out if you did not accompany me. I've become rather used to your constant yammering."

"Speaking of," he said, "did you know that while she was alive, the queen had awful allergies?" asked Hank.

"I . . . what?"

"Because of her severe allergies, the king created an atrium especially for her. It was cleaned top to bottom twice a day and filled with herbs and plants that filtered the air. The queen later added a garden annex to the atrium, and she spent quite a good deal of time there."

"And you think I could do something similar?"

Hank nodded. "Or exactly the same."

During the day, the Netherwood was tacky, but at night it quite literally shone. Neon spiderwebs dotted the canopy, a myriad of brightly colored toadstools grew willy-nilly along the forest floor, and signs flickered and blinked, drawing people in with promises of quick fixes to all life's ails.

Ana sneezed Hank into a bat (better for night flying) and asked him to scout ahead to make sure nothing was amiss, which he happily obliged.

As Ana drew closer to the entrance, she spotted a stomping centaur, her hair and tail dyed a vivid pink, where Penelope had once stood.

"Hi, there," Ana said hesitantly.

"Hello. Was that Hank who just flew overhead?"

Not sure how to respond, as she didn't want Rutle knowing they were there just yet, Ana muttered about bats being common at night.

"I like Hank," the centaur interrupted.

"How do you know him?" Ana asked, intrigued despite herself.

"Oh, well, that's quite depressing, I'm afraid. Hank came to the forest three years ago asking for the cure to a broken heart. Rutle, one of the hags inside these woods, tricked him into signing a contract and immediately turned him into a crow. Sure, he forgot his past life, but it seemed awfully sneaky, if you ask me."

Ana gasped. "You knew Hank when he was human?"

"Not for long. Quite a handsome one, if I recall correctly." She shrugged her shoulders. "Not my type, of course."

Ana smiled despite herself as Hank came flying back out of the woods, landing softly on her outstretched fingers.

"Hiya, Melly," chirped Hank from his upside-down perch. "Melly runs the night shift," he said to Ana. "Might want to call it an early evening," he suggested to the centaur.

Melly yawned and pawed at the ground. "Fair enough," she commented. "I've got a date in an hour, anyway," she said as she began ambling away.

"I suppose I owe you one now," said Hank as the duo followed the signs to Rutle's dementedly bright toadstool.

"Whatever do you mean?" Ana asked, puzzled by the comment.

"I might have spent the rest of my life as a crow, if not for you." Hank paused. "Granted, I won't be able to fly anymore, so I guess you owe me one."

Ana clucked in fake irritation. "So you remember everything now?"

"I do," he said with a stretch of his thin wings. "Most vivid of all, I remember how annoying it is to travel without wings."

Ana could hear Rutle arguing with someone, threatening to turn them into a bugbear if they touched her.

"I suppose that would be one of the fairies?" Ana asked Hank.

Hank nodded his tiny head. "I guess it's time."

Agreeing, Ana pulled from her pocket the large silver summoning pearl that Elidin had given her. Immediately, the golden dragon appeared at her side.

The scaled beast shook her great head and attempted to unfold her wings, screaming out in annoyance when she found them hedged in against her sides by trees.

Elidin glanced at the two of them. "I will wait until I receive word from the fey that the forest has been cleared. The fairies will transport you out shortly." The gold dragon paused before adding, "Thank you. This will be remembered."

Ana opened her mouth to speak but was cut off when Penelope appeared before her in a rush of colored smoke.

"Penelope?" cried Ana. "What are you doing—"

"Your turn!" she interrupted with a smile. The fairy grabbed Ana and transported her to the large field across from the Netherwood, to stand alongside about fifty other creatures. Hags, familiars, customers, and several befuddled centaurs stood milling about, shouting over one another in anger and confusion.

"You were my last charge," Penelope said with a smile. "That felt good!"

"Where is Hank?" Ana asked, looking around for him.

"Oh, no worries, my cousin nabbed him. I specifically asked for you since you saved me."

"Did you organize this?" Ana asked, still a bit bewildered.

"As if. This was all Elidin's doing."

A crashing roar caused the crowd to quiet down and turn back toward the dragon's cry. Great red-hot flames shot into the air, catching the forest ablaze. Leaves shriveled and sizzled into nothing, raining ash onto the ground below. Tree trunks hissed and cracked, splitting apart before bursting into flames.

"The whole forest is on fire!" Ana cried, thinking it wrong to clap happily while people watched their homes burn down.

"And every contract with it," Penelope said smugly.

A man was transported to Ana's left and immediately began calming the angry mob. He announced that this was a raid in the king's name and that all hags would be transported via fairy to the castle dungeons to await trial. Familiars were now free and encouraged to come to court to testify against the hags who had entrapped them.

The dark-headed man also issued a caution about heading back into the wood, as there was a very angry dragon stomping about.

"Excuse me," Ana said, gaining the man's attention, "but who are you?"

He smiled warmly and opened his mouth to speak, but a tiny wail stopped him. To his left, Rutle was in the middle of throttling a fairy to death.

"You blasted tiny thing!" the hag shrieked. "I told you not to touch me!"

"Ana, sneeze!" commanded the man, as he threw yellow sneezing powder into her face.

Fighting her momentary shock, Ana imagined Rutle as a tortoise—slow and harmless—before sneezing. When she opened her eyes, Rutle was, in fact, a gray tortoise. One that hurtled insults and threats at everything around her.

"You would think that would be a humbling experience for her," snarked Penelope.

The fairies wasted no time in profaning the hag's shell with crude graffiti.

Recovering from her delight, Ana rushed toward the man with the sneezing powder. "Hank?" she asked, hoping it was him as he was rather handsome.

"William Hank Bernard the third, actually," he replied.

Ana's mouth fell open. "You're the *prince*?"

He nodded, a crooked smile on his lips. "When my mother died three years ago, I came to this forest to try and forget. I succeeded only in burning half of it down before a wandering hag found me and promised she could ease my suffering."

"Rutle," whispered Ana.

Hank nodded. "My mother's death was heartbreaking, but I was a fool to try and forget."

Ana's mind spun. She had spent the last several weeks with a prince everyone had thought was dead.

"When did you remember you were the prince?"

"Not too terribly long ago," he confessed.

"Why didn't you tell me?" Ana whispered.

"Because you would have insisted on helping me."

"I was going to help you anyway, you dolt!"

"Because I was your friend, not because I was a prince."

"I should change you into an ass," she said hotly.

Hank offered his hand to Ana, smiling cheerfully when she reached out to take it, entwining her fingers with his.

"You're safe now," he promised, pulling her closer to his side.

"I was worried you would be old," Ana admitted with a laugh.

"And I was worried you would hit me for not telling you earlier."

"I still may," she teased.

"Do you remember the room I told you about? The one my father made for my mother?" Hank gently squeezed her fingers.

Ana nodded.

"Would you like to see it?"

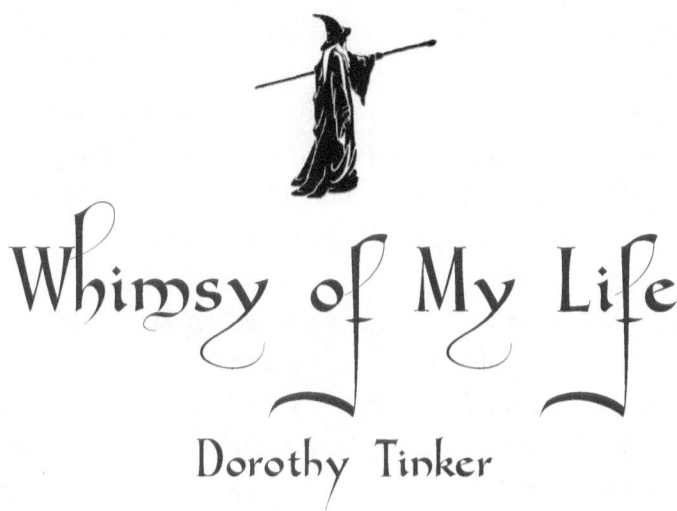

Whimsy of My Life

Dorothy Tinker

I don't dream often.

When I tell people this, they usually retort that I do. I *have* to. It's scientific fact. Everyone has multiple dreams every night; they simply don't remember most of them.

When they say this, I simply smile, nod, and continue whatever conversation led to my claim.

On the inside, though, I'm smirking. Because I know the truth.

I don't dream often, but when I do, the dreams are real and vibrant. And I have yet to forget one.

I was five when I dreamed for the first time. I don't remember being five, but my mother still tells the story of how I grinned and giggled for days after that night. She claims I was five, and if anyone should know, it's her.

Now, I may not remember grinning and giggling and being five when I was awake, but I will never forget that first dream.

I was riding something. Something large and graceful, a creature not of this earth. It shone like a rainbow, its skin/fur/scales soft and nearly nonexistent beneath my fingers.

It was too quick to be a horse, the ride too smooth. I relished its liquid, swinging movements. Closing my eyes, I abandoned myself to the utter joy that slid through me like a long silk ribbon brushing over my soul.

I rode the creature for hours, it seemed, arms stretched wide to accept the blanket of wind that wrapped me up and cradled me like a mother might her babe. The bright sunlight warmed my cheeks and reddened my eyelids, but it was soft enough to welcome my opening eyes without causing them pain.

It was at one of those times, as I opened my eyes to take in the sunlight, that the dream faded like softly drifting mist.

The second dream came when I was nine.

I know this because I had just started fourth grade. The day before I had the dream, the school bully cornered me out of sight of the teachers. I don't remember what he was demanding—my lunch, my homework, it doesn't matter—but I do remember refusing. The only thing I remember after that was the pain and tears and being sent home for fighting.

But more than the measly school bully, I remember the dream that welcomed me when I fell asleep that night.

Warmth. Softness. I was rolling in it. It felt like I had just leaped from the back of whatever creature I had ridden in my previous dream, no matter the years separating the two, to roll in the grass at its feet.

The grass was soft—so soft, it felt like long fur. I could feel each and every strand against my skin, folding in on me and caressing my skin, brushing against would-be bruises and soothing them away.

All the while, I giggled. I laughed. I stretched within the grass's embrace and sighed at its soft touch.

I don't know how long I luxuriated in the grass. It felt like days, lying there in its softness, inhaling the light, sweet scent that just barely touched my nose, tasting the warmth of the breeze that danced daintily and merrily over my bare skin.

It couldn't have been days, though. Not when I had to be at school the next morning. But it felt like it.

Then, when I felt like I could fall asleep among the soft, barely there strands of grass, they curled in just a touch harder, sliding their edges against my sides.

Laughter, oh so joyous, danced from my lungs and lips. I writhed in ticklish pleasure as the grass continued its teasing movements, and my grin felt like it would split my face in two.

I was still laughing when I woke. I remember the odd looks my family wore as they greeted me at breakfast, though not their words.

The kids at school gave me odd looks too. The school bully singled me out again. He demanded to know why I was smiling. I only grinned harder. He must have taken offense at that because he punched me.

I laughed in return. His punch no longer hurt. In fact, the pressure barely tickled, and I had to focus on where his fists were landing to even enjoy that slight pleasure.

He stopped after five punches. He stared at me, his mouth agape, and then turned and ran, screaming that I was crazy.

I didn't care, though. His words meant nothing beside the pleasure I had found in my dream.

I was thirteen when the third dream came. I know because I had just begun to look at other people differently. He was cute, she was pretty, he was handsome, and so on. I had found myself blushing at the most inconvenient times, and it brought teasing and taunting that hurt me in ways fists never had.

The day before I had the third dream, I was played for a fool. Someone asked me out. I can't remember now if it was a girl or a boy, but I do know that person's very presence made me blush and stutter, the breath catching in my throat.

When I finally managed to choke out a yes, the person's earnest smile morphed into a smirk. Other people began to laugh.

"Like I would want to spend time with you!"

Those were the words that broke my heart and sent me to sleep that night with tears in my eyes.

They evaporated like dew on a hot day when I opened my eyes to soft, warm sunlight. The sky above me was a pale purple, the clouds that formed fanciful creatures shining a light crystalline green. The beauty was breathtaking, yet I breathed easily as I took it all in.

I still lay in the fur-like grass, but it no longer tickled me as it had when I was nine. I could hear the deep, even breathing of the creature I had ridden when I was five. It stood/sat/lay some distance beyond my head, but I didn't turn to look. I was too captivated by the sight of the sky.

Until soft touches to my face slowly pulled my attention away from it.

At first, the touches were barely there, just present at the edge of my awareness. Then they grew stronger, outlining the edge of my jaw, curving up around my cheekbones, following the edge of my nose, and sliding over my eyebrows.

I grinned as fingers passed over my eyelids. As they dropped back down to my chin, I opened my eyes and followed the motion with my gaze until I could see the face that belonged to them.

That face was more beautiful than the sky, more beautiful than any person I had ever met in my short life, and more beautiful than anyone I have met since that dream. However humanoid it might have been in shape, I would never limit it by calling it human.

The skin looked infinitely soft, softer even than the grass beneath my back, and it shone with dark light that made it look like liquid wood.

It was the eyes, though, that held me captivated. They shone with an inner radiance, blue, green, gold, silver, black. Any color and every color seemed to shine from those eyes, and they danced merrily beneath my gaze.

"Are you going to lay there all day, then?"

The voice was like music, ranging through tones that no human voice could touch. It made me close my eyes as though to fight back tears, but I knew they wouldn't come.

Maybe, I wanted to answer. I shook my head instead and opened my eyes. The face grinned, and those fingers dropped from my chin to my hand. In one smooth movement, the fingers gripped my own and pulled me to my feet.

The beautiful creature led me, hands still clasped, through the long grass, murmuring softly and pointing to different things.

There was a burbling green river, its current deep and fast, though you couldn't tell it by watching its gentle, melodious surface.

There were jewel-toned mountain peaks, unlike anything I'd ever seen in pictures. They curled and flowed, sometimes upwards, sometimes sideways, but always beautiful in their contours.

Closer at hand, there were trees rising from the soft grassland. Like the mountains, they twisted and curled, but it was their colors that caught my attention. Ivory-colored trunks, like crystalline elephant tusks, tipped with leaves the colors of precious metals: gold, silver, platinum, copper. There were even some with leaves as black as ebony that quivered just slightly in the merry wind.

A hand on my cheek guided my eyes back to that beautiful face, and I had no desire to look away from it. "What do you think?" the musical voice rang. I closed my eyes to enjoy the way it made my insides sing.

Beautiful, I wanted to answer. That word was too simple, though, for how I felt in this being's presence, so I simply smiled.

Something soft brushed my smiling lips. I blinked open my eyes with the hope of catching the creature kissing me, but I opened them only to the growing daylight of my bedroom.

My smile didn't fade, though. The being had kissed me; I was certain of it. It had wanted me, in a way no human ever could.

Reality seemed to pass by in a blur after that. The kids at school quickly gave up their teasing and taunting when I no longer gave them a reaction. Despite the way my heart yearned for my dreams, I continued on with classes and friends and family. The dreams were few and far between, so I just had to go on with life until the next one came.

The fourth dream came when I was eighteen, the night of prom. I didn't go to the dance, not because I wasn't interested in dancing but because there was no one who tempted me. How could I even contemplate a relationship with one of these silly teenage humans when something so much grander and more beautiful waited for me within my dreams?

That night, I fell asleep with an urge to dance and found myself once more in the arms of the beautiful creature.

As I'd thought, its lips were on mine, and they were softer than the touch of a butterfly but so much more present. They were warm too, spreading heat through my chest that might have caused my heart to ache if the creature's presence hadn't soothed it.

When the creature finally pulled away, it smiled, a twist of lips so joyous that an answering joy fluttered within me. It lifted my hand to its lips, kissed the back of it, and whispered words that answered the very desire in my heart.

"Well, then, shall we dance?"

And this person, this creature, this . . . most beautiful being I'd ever met, pulled me close, and we began to twirl.

We danced for hours, listening to the whistle of the wind, the thrumming breath of the rainbow creature that had carried me when I was five, the burbling of the crystalline river, the rumble of the very ground turning beneath our feet. Other sounds joined in the song, so many unusual and varied sounds that I couldn't place their origins, but each addition only heightened the beauty of the song and the joy of the dance.

I was so caught up in the song and the movements that I twirled myself right out of bed when I finally woke. I tumbled to the ground laughing and couldn't care. I had found the creature that fit me best, and nothing could jar me from that realization.

The dreams came more frequently after that, night after night, one endless ephemeral experience after another. I learned more and more of that beautiful, crystalline world, and the more I see of it, the more I crave.

I'm supposed to start college in the fall, but I no longer care about this life. I can't care, not when I think I've finally found a way to trigger the dreams. How can college be important when I no longer have to wait for the dreams to come to me? How can I care about reality when I can chase the rainbow creature and the beautiful being that accompanies it?

Why should I survive the mundane and repetitive when I can strive for the new and overwhelmingly beautiful?

Works of Artifice

Edward Ahern

The off-white tents of the exhibitors were lined up along a harbor-front walkway—paintings and prints, wood and glass wares, pricy knickknacks, food stands. *Art as fast food,* Jason thought.

The paintings reminded him of what he'd tried to achieve and had had to give up on ten years ago. She'd insisted on coming with him.

"Promise me you'll just look, Linda."

"What's the point of just looking?"

Jason felt his face redden. "We don't have the money to spend. You know how far underwater we are."

His voice was too loud, hers too shrill, and the vendor in the tent in front of them turned away to fiddle with his display of pens.

"You miser. Just get a better job."

"Please, Linda, I'm begging you. Don't buy anything; just look. We can't even make minimum payments on the credit cards."

She waved a plump arm. "You depress me. I'm going for a walk around on my own. You do the same. And get a life we can live."

Jason's skin felt like it was going to split. He breathed heavily for a minute. *Bitch.*

He browsed in the direction opposite the one Linda had taken. Dressed like the underperforming salesman he was, he was largely ignored by the artists manning the booths.

Some of these paintings are beautiful, but who can pay $2,300 for an oil small enough to fit in a bathroom? I should've been a painter. I had talent. I shouldn't have brought her.

A beet-colored tent caught his eye, and he walked into it. The paintings inside were washed in crimson light. The styles were different, but the approach to the subjects was common—subversion of the bland into the just discernably grotesque.

Jason paused in front of a painting of a man and woman working in a fruit orchard. The trees were blighted and the fruit wizened. They faced outward with strained expressions, and Jason wondered if it was work stress or if they despised each other. The perverse scene was achingly well-executed.

"One of my favorites too."

Jason spun around to face a stoop-backed old man. "Ah, hello. Yes, it's interesting. Distorted though."

The old man's smile spread like an oil slick. "I don't see distortion. I see what's painfully real underneath the cosmetics we slather on life."

"Just curious, how much is this one?"

"It's $3,500."

Peculiar and expensive. I can't even afford a pay-per-view movie; leave it be. He's right, though. It's true to life.

"Thanks. Think I'll keep browsing."

"Let me show you around. That still life on the left, the showy flowers past their prime. What do you see?"

Jason moved closer to the picture. "There's flawed opulence in them. The artist has applied the colors like they were seeping from wounds."

The old man smiled again. "You've had artistic training. A painter, I think. This little one here, the sleeping dog. But is it?"

Jason nodded. "The mange, the scabby nose, the uncomfortable posture. A brutal depiction, makes me think of a bitter elderly relative. A question, though. They're unsigned, but the styles and brush strokes are different. Is there more than one artist?"

"A discerning question. Let's sit over there in the folding chairs while I explain."

As Jason stepped over to a chair, he wrinkled his nose. The aromas wafting off the paintings reminded him of rotting plants.

"There, that's better," the old man said. "Yes, the art is done by apprentices who've accepted my guidance. They've become possessed of my vision of the bitter truths of life. We cast out the self-flagellating fables of pretty and good."

"Refreshing, but please don't try to sell me on them. I can barely afford to look."

The old man's face wrinkled into billows of gray. "Wait, sit still. Let me show you something."

He hopped up, went to the back of the tent, and pulled an unframed oil from a stack of paintings leaning against a tent pole. "Here," he said as he came back and sat down. "Here's one of my own compositions. I'd appreciate your opinion."

Jason stared at a thirtyish-year-old woman standing in a room crowded with furniture and bric-a-brac. She was smirking, exultant. Coarse emotions rampaged over her face. Beneath the grin, Jason sensed hate. "It's wonderful," he said. "Congratulations."

"It's yours."

Jason checked his irritation. "I told you, I can't buy it."

"No, listen. You can pay for it in artwork. I'll even pay you a generous stipend."

"What?"

"You'd just have to become my apprentice."

"I haven't painted in years."

"I'll instruct you. The materials and teaching are free. You already share my cynicism; just contribute to my cause."

Jason almost choked on his words. "I'd love to, God help me, but I've got enough problems without taking on an all-consuming vocation."

"You'll be able to do much more than paint. I'll help change your life."

Just then, Linda stuck her head in the tent. "There you are." She was grinning, holding a decorated bag with *Shaw's Jewelers* printed in big letters. "I'm afraid I've been a bad girl."

Alongside Linda, the man and woman in the orchard stared back at Jason. Their faces looked frightened.

Jason's lips tightened. "Have you now?" He turned to the old man. "You see why I can't do what you ask?"

Teeth showed in the old man's smile. "On the contrary. I'll show you how to remove your limitations."

Linda shrilled, "Jason, let's go."

Jason turned to face her. "No, Linda, not yet." He turned back to the old man. "All of them? There's always a cost. What do you get out of this?"

"You won't pay any money, and what you lose you've never noticed. What I receive is a convert to my beliefs. Will you follow me?"

"Hell yes."

The King of the Frogs

Kelly Lynn Colby

Rufus, the king of the frogs, wished to change the reputation of his people. Every time a witch punished a vain prince, she turned him into a frog, like that was the worst thing she could imagine.

A slight bump to his lily pad drew Rufus's attention.

"Your Majesty." Harold, the king's most trusted steward, bowed from the edge of the royal lily pad.

Well, this year's royal lily pad. It changed often depending on the winter and which plant grew the largest. A lovely willow tree shaded this one as the sun set. Rufus hoped it would remain there for the whole season.

Harold cleared his throat.

"Yes, Harold, what needs tending to?" King Rufus stared across the green surface at his steward perched on the end.

"It's the new prince, Your Majesty."

"He's adjusting well and wishes to never return to his parched, noisy life in the town, right?" Rufus chuckled to himself. He was such a funny frog.

Harold looked down at the lily pad. "No, Your Majesty. He says he can't swim and refuses to wet more than his feet."

"Did you inform the dimwit that he's a frog now and frogs can swim?" The king caught a mosquito with a quick flick of his tongue.

He was stress eating again. Harold would be very unhappy if the servants had to dig a larger hole to winter in.

"We've tried to make it abundantly clear."

Rufus searched for another bite. A dragonfly flew close. The king dismissed the crunchy treat. It would take him too long to swallow the larger insect. He had to deal with this prince. "Did you tell the dunce that he'll get dizzy and weak from lack of air if he doesn't keep his skin moist?"

"We've done our utmost to be clear, Your Majesty."

The king nodded his head up and down. The rattle of the crown perched between his bulbous eyes helped him think. "Toss him in the pond."

"Yes, Your Majesty." Harold's lips tweaked up at the ends. "As you wish."

"Oh, and Steward Harold, warn the prince to avoid the catfish. We don't want a repeat of Prince Winston's fate."

That hadn't been a fun time to be king. Newly turned Prince Winston had swum to the bottom of the pond to hide from a cockroach. Of all things! He'd refused to listen to his frog acclimators. A catfish had swallowed him whole before he'd had the joy of crunching through his first fly. Such a waste.

When his father, King Trudeau, had come to the swamp to find his cursed son, the steward had confessed the prince's demise before Rufus could make up an alternative scenario. Luckily, the king of the frogs was as smart as he was funny. He didn't want the humans to dredge the bottom of his pond to find the catfish murderer. His poor kingdom would never recover.

So he had lied.

Rufus had spun the tale of a hungry wolf threatening the life of Rufus's daughter. Winston bravely hopped between the mighty canine jaws and the terrified princess. The wolf took Winston and cantered off into the woods.

Even though wolves don't eat frogs, the grieving father had bought the tale. Humans hate wolves as a rule. It was an easy lie to sell.

And Rufus had no daughters. Or sons. Not because they were eaten by wolves (see above on wolf-frog relations). He'd simply never found the queen of his heart.

"Of course, Your Majesty." Harold flattened his body against the lily pad. He pushed with his back legs to slide into the water with minimal splashing.

King Rufus hiccuped his appreciation for the new procedure. He'd grown tired of the departing deluge of his servants washing his crown from his head. Before Rufus could speak with his next appointment, the crown would have to be dug up from the bottom of the pond and scrubbed with a cattail brush. The process used to make his nights last so long, he'd miss the delicious fireflies. What was the point of being king if he didn't get his pick of the nightly feast?

He snapped a freshly shed cicada from a branch of the willow. Rufus needed to keep his energy up for the rest of his kingly duties.

Stewart, the royal herald, hopped onto the lily pad. The king hadn't been expecting him tonight.

"Do we have a visitor? I don't remember anything on the calendar." Rufus burped. Cicadas were best when they lost their tough nymph exoskeleton.

"Your Majesty, Princess Helen of Lovely Land has come to find her prince and asks your permission to kiss your subjects." Stewart blinked one eye as the wind blew seeds from the willow into the air.

Rufus blinked one eye in surprise. "A human princess is asking permission? That's a nice change." His community relations must be working. "Who's up for kissing duty?" A selection seemed to satisfy the picky princesses, who were never happy if the first frog they kissed transformed before their eyes. They always asked whether there was a better one out there. But by then, it would be too late. Each princess only received one magic kiss. In all his years as ruler, Rufus had never seen a princess able to transform more than one cursed human.

"Terrence, Leslie, Kolleen, and Colin."

To ensure his kingdom rid themselves of the frogified prince of their choosing, the king had been manipulating the selection process for years. "Excellent. And the prince you have in mind?"

"Prince Baudouin, Your Majesty." The herald then croaked as something bumped the bottom of the lily pad.

The king of the frogs rolled his eyes at Stewart's fear. No predator from the deep would ever be allowed to harm him. His guards were too good.

Rufus kicked his back legs against the pliable surface. Signal waves rushed from all sides of the floating leaf. The head of the guard amplified the waves with his own stomping on a nearby pad. Six splashes echoed under the willow branches as the six largest, meanest bullfrogs in the kingdom swam to the aid of their king.

Refusing to let the interloper disturb his workday, Rufus whacked Stewart with his tongue. The herald croaked again, this time emptying his cloaca. The mess in the middle of the royal court on the royal lily pad was completely unacceptable.

The king closed his inner eyelids. As much as it amused him to have a herald named Stewart and a steward name Harold, it might be time to interview for a new herald. He might be a bit too jumpy for this important role.

For now, Rufus chose to ignore Stewart's misstep as he ignored the commotion under his feet. "Prince Baudouin hasn't changed at all. He still spends too much time staring at himself in dew drops and braiding grass as a wig. This princess was polite enough to beg my leave. I wish to reward her with a good catch."

Rufus scratched under his chin as he imagined great human kings did. "Prince Liam of Grassy Lowlands has been an asset to our kingdom. It should be him."

The herald straightened his neck, trying to regain some dignity. "Of course, Your Majesty. But he is away leading the kitchen experiment."

"You see, an asset! He should be reporting back soon. Ask the princess to return in two nights' time and we will have her prince."

Stewart hesitated at the edge of the lily pad. King Rufus knew he feared entering the water until the guards had dealt with the intruder. If he pushed the herald in, would he be a good king or a bad king? He would certainly be a funny king.

The bustle under the water quieted as his burly guards hauled a netted catfish to the containment hole on the shore. Rufus tapped his thin nails on the pad in his excitement. It was he who had taught the populace to make nets to capture predators. With their tiny hands tying the most intricate knots, the frog nets became the most demanded fishing tool in all Windfern. The straw weavers delivered strong magical string by the bushel to keep up with demand.

A gentle rocking told Rufus the herald had dismounted the lily pad. The king took the opportunity to jump off his soiled pad to swim to shore. Two splashes on either side echoed his. Never alone, but always lonely. It was odd being king.

With the water on the surface still warm from the day's sun, Rufus dove deeper to reach a cooler layer. His strokes were a bit awkward since he had to use one leg to hold his crown in place. There were so many trials as king. Invigorated by the swim and the comforting temperatures, he surfaced and paddled his way to shore.

"Your Majesty." Six beefy frogs bowed as low as their massive chests would allow.

Rufus returned the gesture and peered into the catfish containment. "That's a big one. Princess Tatiana will be pleased."

Princess Tatiana visited Rufus at least once a week. The catfish holding pond had been dug just for her to collect her favorite treat. The king's three-chambered heart picked up an odd rhythm at the thought of her messy brown hair and permanently smiling eyes. There was something about her that reminded him of something he couldn't remember.

The guards tensed as a stork landed in the shallow water by the shore. Rufus crouched, ready to slide under the tree roots if necessary. Two deep-red stripes flashed in the last bit of the dying sun.

Rufus let out his breath as his guards relaxed. "Beatrice, sweet girl. What have you brought me this evening?"

Beatrice used to be a nursemaid, then nanny, for a human prince. When a witch cursed her beloved charge, she begged the magic user to turn her too, so she could continue to care for him. The evil witch, having a wicked sense of humor, transformed Beatrice into a stork, one of the largest devourers of frogs in Windfern. But the nursemaid had had the last laugh. She retained enough of her old self to morph into the only vegetarian stork.

Over the years, Beatrice became an asset to the frog kingdom, offering easy transport to far away castles.

Today, her pointy beak held a basket that jerked back and forth with the exaggerated movements of her head.

"Put me down before I break your beak."

"Jolene?" Rufus knew that angry voice. "Put the basket down, Beatrice. Good girl."

As soon as the bottom of the basket touched the ground, Jolene, one of his best emissaries, hopped out.

Rufus snapped his tongue at one of his guards. "See to it that a plate of morsels is brought at once." He didn't like the pale-green skin of his normally emerald-green ambassador. "How did it go with the witches?"

Jolene shook her head in a very human way. "I don't know. They were willing to speak with me, but they seemed too concerned with their own problems to make the rebels of their order respect the frog kingdom."

"Did you tell them we could supply them with rare herbs found only in our swamp?" The king motioned to another servant to splash water on Jolene's parched skin.

The beleaguered ambassador sighed in relief as her voice grew stronger. "That's the only reason they agreed to speak with me. They said they would consider my offer, but I wouldn't sit in the sun. There could be quite a wait."

Rufus huffed. He snagged a mosquito from behind Jolene as she grabbed one from behind him.

He had so many questions. "Did you at least find out why they turn princes into frogs, while they make princesses fall into deep sleeps?"

Jolene rolled her eyes in different directions. "I don't think witches are capable of independent thought. The first witch did it the first time, and now that's what they all do."

"Primitive."

"I know." Jolene buried her belly in the cool mud.

Rufus saw the exhaustion etched on her face. He nodded in approval at his guards as they arrived carrying a woven net full of grubs. His stablers brought stocks of wheat for Beatrice.

"You rest. We'll search the reeds for more ideas tomorrow." Rufus was wise and funny and generous. The frog kingdom was lucky to have him.

Jolene burped. "Maybe you should talk to Chelydra the Ancient."

The king tripped mid-hop at the dreaded reference. "No, I don't want to talk to that slack-jawed slowpoke. Once a reign is enough."

"But . . ."

"Eat your dinner. I have business elsewhere." Rufus resumed his royal leaping. He'd sooner allow himself to be covered in fly feces than have to ask advice from Chelydra the Ancient.

The king of the frogs ignored the echoing hops behind him. He wished to stomp off on his own but knew better than to order his shadows away. That was the one command that would not be obeyed by any of his royal guardians, not while he was out in the open anyway.

Warmth escaped the pond water, creating a muggy mist. Frog heaven. He tilted his head toward the cypress tree he was aiming for. Its roots stuck above the stickiest, most well-maintained mud in the kingdom. Madam Tumi made sure of it.

A rotund frog, with a face so fat that her eyes looked half the size of a typical amphibian's, swaggered in an unfrog-like manner toward her honored guest. "Your Majesty." She bowed deeply, her layers flattening, blocking the entryway. The relaxing scent of lavender floated on top of the alluring sweet-sour of the mud. "Your usual spot awaits."

"Thank you, Madam Tumi. It is, as always, my pleasure to see you again." Rufus centered his crown, which had shifted in all the hopping.

The large frog practically rolled to the side to allow the king and his guards to squeeze through the above-ground cypress roots. She thumped her back foot on the ground three times. A group of attendants surrounded the king.

Freshly rubbed down, King Rufus sank into his cool pool. The weight of the sticky, lavender-scented mud relaxed the amphibian. His eyelids lowered as his stress melted away. He drifted into a dreamlike state.

He lay in a large four-poster bed with a giggling little human girl beside him. Her brown curls and sparkling eyes bounced in glee as he pretended to be annoyed with her and demanded she go back to her own room.

"Your Majesty! Your Majesty!"

Rufus pushed out of the muck, his mood ruined by the urgent interruption. "Can't the cursed kingdom get along without me for an hour?"

"Your Majesty." Sir Liam bowed; his entire body shook, producing a jiggling in the mud.

Before Rufus's anger could overtake his royal calm, he realized Liam wasn't supposed to return for another week. The king shook off what was left of his drowsiness. "What happened in the kitchens at the Newberry castle?"

Sir Liam pushed away an attendant who was trying to sponge his dusty skin. "At first, everything went splendidly. We showed the cook that frogs could make great fly control."

Rufus touched his crown, though it hadn't moved. "At first?"

"Yes, everyone was happy. Our entourage from the Frog Kingdom was well fed and instances of maggoty meat declined significantly. I thought we were finally making headway in frog-human camaraderie. But then . . . ." Liam's green complexion faded to a dry-grass brown.

"But?" King Rufus blinked furiously.

"A couple of weeks later, the humans said we did a good job. They looked pleased." Liam swallowed a gulp of air. It escaped through his vocal cords with a loud croak. "The kitchen staff decided the fly problem was no more and we weren't needed. A bit disappointed but proud we had accomplished our goal, we packed to go home."

Another hard swallow.

King Rufus smacked the knight with his tongue. "Get yourself together. What happened?"

"The cook snatched us into a net and dumped us into a pot of water."

Rufus's skin mirrored the faded dry-grass brown of his knight. "She wouldn't dare."

"But she did. She said the regent wished for frog legs for dinner that night and what the regent wants, the regent gets."

"How did you escape?" Rufus's muscles tightened, squeezing blood into his brain. The mud pile did nothing to soothe his righteous anger.

"Luckily, we had made friends with the kitchen mice. They caused a distraction and chewed through the net. We were able to hop out before the water boiled."

"Those humans can dry in the desert for their treachery!" Rufus thumped his back foot on the clay around the mud.

Madam Tumi moved much quicker than her bulk seemed to allow. She bowed before her king.

"Madam Tumi, make sure Sir Liam and his entourage are properly tended to. Send the bill to the treasury." Rufus shook his body to remove the excess mud. Attendants jumped to attention and dried off what they could before spraying him with scented slug mucus.

As he forced himself to sit still for the treatment, his mind raced for a solution. "What can we do?" Rufus addressed one of his guards, who understood that the question was rhetorical. The king often talked to himself to work through a conundrum.

Sir Liam, however, didn't know that. He turned at the entrance of another room. "We could confer with Chelydra the Ancient. He has lived through war with the humans before."

"What is it with that rock-skinned buffoon? All he does is stand there with his mouth open all day. He wouldn't know the first thing about frog-human relations." King Rufus hopped away before Liam could offer any other mosquito-brained suggestions. A creature didn't become wise simply by living longer.

He hopped in the direction of the royal lily pad. He needed time to think, and the steward would keep everyone at bay while he did exactly that.

"King Rufus!"

"Princess Tatiana!" The ends of Rufus's lips twisted up so far, they tickled his secondary eyelids. The princess was the only human Rufus had ever met who could tell the frogs apart. Her cheerful outlook was exactly what he needed on this most disappointing of days. He hurried his pace to the willow tree. "We have the most decadent catfish for you. I think you will be most—"

The girl sat crossed-legged at the base of the tree. Her dress, normally caked in mud, sparkled the most pristine white. Her dark hair, which normally stuck out from her head in an unruly mess, twisted in elaborate braids. Her face, normally glowing with robust cheer, melted into soggy sadness.

"Oh, King Rufus, the most horrible thing is happening. I don't know what to do. I am the heir. I should be obeyed, but they only scoff at my youth and lack of a husband." The human girl bent in half over her lap. The most terrible noise, nothing like her usual giggling laughter, poured from the shivering bundle.

For all his wit and wisdom, the king of the frogs didn't know how to comfort her. And he didn't know why her sadness bothered him so deeply.

"Sweet Princess Tatiana, why do you cry so?" Harold crawled out of the pond and blinked one eye at his king. He stomped on the ground and croaked three notes. A fluttering in the tree announced the arrival of the lightning bug squad. For a promise of amnesty, one family of glow-in-the-dark bugs agreed to act as light for the royal court. Though frogs had pretty good night vision, some of their guests had none.

"Harold?" Tatiana lifted her head. She wiped her eyes with the hem of her skirt. "I'm sorry. I've been crying for hours now. I was forbidden from coming to see you, but I snuck out."

Rufus had missed the absence of her guards and nanny. "That's very dangerous. What happens if you run into trouble without your trusted guards?"

"Plus, your men will now be punished for losing you." Harold slurped up a passing mosquito.

Another benefit to the lightning bug squad. They attracted the crunchy little treats. Rufus joined in on the feast while leaving one eye focused on the princess.

Tatiana pulled her knees to her chest. "It was important. I had to warn you." She swatted a mosquito on her arm. Rufus scowled at the wasted meal. "Regent Aleister has made a deal with the neighboring kingdom to build a bridge through the swamp to ease trade."

Rufus's mosquito-filled stomach squirmed. "He can't do that. We're a sovereign kingdom."

Tatiana nodded. "That's what I said, and I refused to sign the treaty. But Regent Aleister just laughed at me. He said they don't need my permission because I'm not of legal age. He said, what are the frogs going to do, ribbit us to death? Then . . ."

A deep croak escaped from Rufus before he could stop it. His eyeballs bulged more than usual as his three-chambered heart pumped furiously.

Bending down to cry again, Tatiana couldn't continue.

"Come now, dear, you are royalty." Rufus straightened his front legs and lifted his meager chin as high as his bulbous neck would allow.

Tatiana sniffed and wiped her eyes again. She straightened her back and lifted her chin like a pasty caricature of the king. "My mom died at my birth. My father disappeared when I was three. I've sat on the throne since, but it's only been for show. Regent Aleister's signature is the only one that counts until I come of age."

One of Harold's eyes looked at his king, while the other stayed focused on the princess. "When do you come of age, dear?"

"In one year." Tatiana took a deep breath and swallowed. "By the time I have the power to stop the bridge, Aleister will have drained the swamp."

"Princess Tatiana, we are grateful you have brought us this news."

Rufus joined his steward beside the girl. "The night moves on, and you must return to your family."

Tatiana sprang up. "But I want to help!" The frogs jumped out of the way of her nervous feet.

Rufus soothed her. "You *have* helped, princess. Now go home and let us worry about protecting our kingdom."

Before the amphibians could protest, Tatiana scooped them into her hands and cuddled the creatures against her cheeks. Rufus held his crown with one foot and fought the nausea of the undignified jostling. Instead of losing his stomach contents, Rufus reveled in the feel of the human's soft, wartless skin and the smell of roses. A peace more powerful than he'd ever felt with the lavender and mud at Madam Tumi's sank into his soul.

Tatiana placed them gently on the ground. For a moment, Rufus felt cold and abandoned.

Mud coated the back of Tatiana's dress as she scampered under the willow branches to the road beyond. That was the way it was supposed to look.

After her tall form disappeared into the dark, the steward turned to his king. "You could speak with—"

Rufus interrupted him. "I think I'll go speak with Chelydra the Ancient."

Harold bowed. "You are a wise king."

The king of the frogs swam to the grassy island in the center of the swamp. His eyes hovered just above the water's surface, his crown settled between the two bulbous protrusions.

"You four, wait here," Rufus said to his guards without looking at them.

Croaking among the bullfrogs indicated they weren't happy with their king's command. Rufus ignored them as he hopped to shore. He was wise and knew what to do. A deep rivet from a spikey tail led him to a rotting log.

In front of the decaying wood lay a giant mottled dome. Lichen grew along its bumpy surface, which peaked in the middle. Square sections of mini mountain peaks crossed in concentric circles. A dark cave loomed ominously under an outcropping.

Straightening his crown before addressing the seer, Rufus stared into the void. The moonless night offered no insight into what lurked inside.

But King Rufus didn't need the light. He was wise, after all. No fear hindered his call to Chelydra.

It was just the speech. The silly, mostly annoying, definitely humiliating phrases he had to recite for the reptile to even consider speaking with the king of the frogs. That was the real reason he didn't want his guards to follow. He'd never live it down.

He cleared his throat with a mighty croak. "Oh, Great Chelydra the Ancient, keeper of the forgotten text, rememberer of times long past, predictor of future events, and . . ." Rufus swallowed hard. "Best frog king rescuer in all the kingdoms."

Rufus despised that last line. He'd gotten a little tangled in a fish net once, and Chelydra happened to know how to free him. So now, for the rest of his reign, he had to be embarrassed by this hard-shelled cretin.

Out of the cave shot an impossibly long neck. The sharp beak on the end snapped closed a mere fly's leg from the king's snout. Rufus tightened his cloaca. He refused to show fear before this predator's grandstanding. He was still the king. If anything happened to him, snapping turtle or no, Chelydra's life would be forfeit.

Tiny eyes lost in the folds of old age focused on Rufus's crown. "You still insist on donning that relic." Chelydra's deep voice vibrated through the frog's limbs.

"Look, you old reptile, I *have* to wear the crown. I am the king of the frogs." Rufus straightened his shoulders and glared back.

Chelydra laughed. At least, that's how Rufus interpreted the vibrating shell that shook the ground beneath his feet.

How dare he? The king dug his nails into the damp dirt, like a cat ready to pounce.

The king of the frogs ribbited to clear his throat. "The Regent of Thorta has made a deal with the king of Theron to build a bridge through the frog kingdom. I need to know how to stop them from draining my swamp and killing everyone in it." Afraid Chelydra might refuse to help, he added, "Which would affect you too. Where would you be without the swamp?"

Rufus closed both his eyelids as a stinky puff of fish stench blew from the turtle's nostrils.

Chelydra said, "There is but one way."

The giant snapping turtle extended his cypress-root-sized feet from their holes in his shell. Slowly lifting his bulk from the damp earth, he rotated until his tail swung toward Rufus's jaw. The frog jumped, successfully clearing the wormy limb before it hit him. Rufus was wise and funny and athletic.

Chelydra turned back around with a piece of yellowed parchment covered in black mildew spots. A faded drawing of a young human king covered the center of the announcement. He looked familiar. His dark curly hair and pointed nose and chin reminded Rufus of someone.

"Tatiana. He looks like the princess."

"That is because he is her father."

Rufus took the parchment from the turtle. A reward of a thousand gold pieces was offered for the safe return of the missing King of Thorta. "How is this helpful?"

"You must find him." Chelydra peered over the notice like a looming deity. "You are the only one who can."

Rufus rolled his eyes in opposite directions. "I knew this was a mistake. You have no idea how to help me, do you?" Sending the king of the frogs to find a missing-for-over-a-decade king of the humans. Ridiculous.

Chelydra plunked down in the moist mud. "He is one of the no-names."

"The no-names?" Rufus shivered. One witch, no one knew her name for sure, used to transform princes, kings, knights, queens, chancellors, and anyone else of power who displeased her into frogs with no memories of who they had been before that moment. She was eventually caught and stripped of her powers by her fellow witches. Even without magic though, the mysterious witch was still smarter than her sisters by far. She had managed to escape into the haunted forest, taking her secrets with her.

The swamp had a couple dozen no-name frogs. "One of the no-names? But how do I know which one?"

"You are the only one who can find him. Use your resources wisely." Chelydra sucked in a torrent of air in a mighty yawn.

Rufus leaned back to avoid getting pulled toward the predator's jaws. "That's not very useful, you know. What resources? Beautiful wart-filled frog forms look nothing like pasty human ones. This picture does me no good. I . . ." He wanted to stomp his feet and eat something.

Chelydra pulled his head into his shell with a thunk. From under the scalloped edge, his voice sounded far away. "Find the king."

Rufus grumbled to himself for the entire swim back to his lily pad. How was he to find the right frog? And once he did, how would he turn him back without a princess to kiss him? What if he still had no memory of who he was after he was transformed?

Once he returned home, he immediately sent for his herald. Rufus would gather the no-names. One problem at a time.

Stewart bowed before his king. "Yes, Your Majesty."

"I need you to announce the congregation of all the no-names in the kingdom. We need them assembled under the willow tree as quickly as possible. You have access to all the guards and any other citizens you must enlist."

Stewart blanched, the typical reaction to the no-names. "As you command, Your Majesty."

Now to find a princess willing to kiss for the greater good. He could start with Princess Tatiana. Surely she would be on board with the search for her father. Since she could tell the frogs apart, maybe, just maybe, she would know which one was her father.

Rufus called for his steward.

Harold bowed before his king. "Yes, Your Majesty."

"I need you to take Beatrice to Thorta Castle and beg an audience with Princess Tatiana. I kindly request a visit at her earliest convenience." Rufus released some of his anxiety in a loud burp. "Please make sure she understands the urgency of my request without letting on about our plans to the Regent's men."

"Of course, Your Majesty." Harold hopped off the lily pad, forgetting the new procedure.

The splashed water toppled the king's crown off his head. He snagged it with his tongue before it could plunge into the water. Rufus put the symbol of his authority back on but didn't take the time to make sure it was perfectly straight. Too many other responsibilities pulled at his mind. He needed a plan B—something to protect his kingdom if the search for the lost king failed.

Across the lawn of lily pads, Rufus spotted a group of his citizens weaving a net. Too bad the kingdom hadn't earned enough from this grand invention to bribe the kingdoms to avoid his swamp.

Avoid his swamp? Humans built roads around the Haunted Forest rather than cut through the middle of it because of rumors of its supernatural nature. What if Rufus created the same illusion for his kingdom? If the swamp was perceived as haunted, the humans would leave him and his people alone. The witches might even stop turning princes into frogs to avoid the entire area. This could solve all his problems.

He summoned the frog council.

Princess Tatiana slid off her roan, straight to her knees before the king of the frogs. "Oh, King Rufus, is it true? Can you find my father?"

For a moment, Rufus felt guilty for raising her hopes. He was trusting the word of a senile snapping turtle. He would roast that old fool if he was making it all up and caused any pain to the princess.

"I hope so. But I can't do it without your help."

Rufus croaked. Stewart the herald hopped forward, followed by a group of confused frogs. A group of frustrated guards herded them forward like mice trying to roll their acorns in a straight line. Some of the no-names looked terrified, but most seemed oblivious.

"Is my father one of these frogs?" Tatiana's voice rose at the end.

Rufus nodded. He nervously sucked up three insects one flap of his tongue. "Choose wisely."

Tatiana swallowed hard and wiped an errant tear from her cheek. "I better start kissing."

Rufus jumped in front of her. "Actually, Princess Tatiana, your kiss will only work once. I was hoping you would be able to identify which one is the human king, your father."

"Could the witches be any crueler?" Tatiana brushed a tear away. "You expect me to find my father among this selection?"

"You are the only human I've ever known who can tell us apart. If anyone can do it, it's you."

Tatiana put her hand down for Rufus to hop onto. Eye-to-eye, they stared at each other.

"Okay, I'll try." The princess kissed Rufus on his cheek.

The king of the frogs recoiled as a shock zapped his body. Tatiana had touched him many times before, and it had never hurt. His vision blurred and his limbs tingled. The king's stomach twisted worse than when he had swallowed that wasp. *My crown,* he thought as the precious possession rolled off his head, but he couldn't move to stop it.

Princess Tatiana dropped him and backed against the willow's trunk.

King Rufus tried to comfort her, but he couldn't talk. A buzzing swelled in his head, accompanied by voices—human voices.

"You ridiculous king with your ridiculous rules. You cannot forbid me from harvesting any herb I desire from the frog kingdom. They are amphibians. What

rights do they have?" A wretched witch smelling of mildew and unwashed socks stood before the throne of a king.

A robust voice, familiar yet foreign, came from the throne. "Witch, you will do as you are ordered. That land belongs to the frogs, and you witches tamper with their sovereignty enough. I won't have you trampling their pristine swamp to obtain herbs with dubious intent."

The witch bowed without lowering her head. The green-flecked brown of her irises bore into Rufus's soul. "Of course, Your Majesty."

Pain arced from his toes, to his back, to his tongue. No part of his body was free from the grip of agony.

Every nerve in his body grew agitated, finding places to cause pain he hadn't known he had. He looked down in horror as his skin smoothed and lost its healthy green. His bulbous eyes sunk into his head, along with his protruding nose. His tongue—no, not his tongue. The thick, strong means for keeping him fed shrunk to a pathetically useless appendage.

He was transforming. He'd seen it so many times as king of the frogs that the event was no longer remarkable.

Until now.

With one last deafening pop, the agony dissipated. Rufus lay prone on the ground, exhausted. He tried to take in his surroundings, but he felt handicapped because his eyes refused to move independently. How did humans get around?

"King Rufus?" Tatiana's voice sounded different to his new ears. She knelt beside him. "Father?"

He rolled forward to see his reflection in the pond. With brown curls and a pointed nose and chin, he looked just like the drawing of the missing sovereign. He squeezed his eyes shut as a flood of repressed memories rushed through him.

"Your Highness, what a surprise to see you here." The witch smiled at the king like she was ready to eat him.

King Rudolph of Thorta squinted at the wrinkled creature. "What are you doing in the swamp? I warned you about trespassing. Guards!"

"Oh, no, you don't." A flash arced from the witch's walking stick. Pain

ripped through his body as his mass dropped to a fraction of its original. His mind felt light, scrubbed, erased.

"Your Majesty?" Two guards jumped from the bushes.

The tallest held his spear at the witch's throat. "Where is our sovereign?"

"I have not seen any humans this day besides you two." She picked up the freshly transformed frog and placed him on a large toadstool. She snapped her fingers, and a tiny crown appeared. She placed it on the new frog's head. "This is Rufus, king of the frogs. Maybe he knows."

"Your Majesty." Both men bowed to the blinking frog as the witch slipped into the weeds.

All this time, he had been one of the no-names. Rudolph/Rufus sat with crossed legs as he'd seen Tatiana do many times. It felt unnatural. He'd adjust. He was wise and funny and athletic, after all.

Tatiana pulled her shawl from her shoulders. "I don't understand."

Rufus gratefully tied the silky cloth around his waist. "I remember. How could I forget? The witch cursed me. I was trying to protect the swamp, so she made me its sovereign."

"I can't believe you're back." Tatiana twisted his curls between her fingers.

He heard a ruckus near the cypress mud pits. The amphibians were carrying out the attack without him. Good.

"I have one last duty to perform as king of the frogs. I must defend this land from the invading humans." He ran into the woods.

Tatiana dashed after him. "Not without me, you're not."

Rudolph stopped and grabbed her hand. "Let's go, then, my daughter. King of the frogs and his brave daughter, united for the good of both kingdoms."

Unraveled

Kelsey Dean

Buying the bath mat had been a bad idea. A very bad idea. Arguably the worst joint decision that Mike and Melika had ever made. And that was saying something; on their own, both were terrible decision makers. Combined, they were even worse. It had taken months, and an intervention by their wedding party, to decide on a honeymoon location, and they still hadn't settled on an internet provider by the time they were married.

"Dina was right about this place," Melika said with a dreamy smile as they strolled through the streets of Istanbul arm in arm. Their wedding rings twinkled in the late afternoon sun, and Mike ran a thumb over his, still adjusting to the feel of the silver band on his finger. Melika grinned at him and gave his arm a squeeze.

"I can't get enough of these windows," Mike said, pointing to a towering display of baklava. Honey dripped from the feathery edges and landed in a golden lake that spread outward in slow motion. The next shop they passed boasted a wall of colorful cubes that glowed like gemstones: Turkish delight. They were clustered according to flavor and adorned with emerald pistachios, rose petals, and snowy coconut shavings.

Melika's teeth ached; every sweet shop they passed bombarded them with samples of decadent candies. Mike took yet another from a smiling man with a tray.

"Yes, please," said the man as he offered the tray to Melika.

"No, thank you," she replied.

"Very delicious," insisted the man. Mike shrugged and took another. They hurried away as he invited them inside, offering tea and discounts.

"Gift boxes, very good price!"

The Turkish delight man's shouts faded into a dozen others, all calling out deals and offers in a mixed cacophony of languages, appealing to locals and tourists alike.

By the fifth day of their honeymoon, Mike and Melika were proud that they had agreed on a small handful of souvenirs to bring home. Just one fez, a couple of hand-painted plates, and as thank-you tokens for their entire wedding party, a small bag of key chains sporting abstract eyes made of blue glass.

"Very smart," said the little lady who sold them the glass charms. "Protection against the evil eye. Important for newlyweds."

Melika decided that there was something else important for newlyweds to acquire on their honeymoon: a practical, everyday object to use around the house and remind them of the first days of their marriage.

Mike pointed toward the window of a little shop near their hotel: Baba Mudi's Bath Mats. The awning spelled it out invitingly in curly crimson letters that had beckoned to them every time they walked by. Baba Mudi himself grinned and waved at passersby from the doorway at any hour of the day or night. If there were people on the street, he was there, enticing them into his shop with his booming voice. He was jolly, with a round belly and a frizzy grey beard, and he was constantly wreathed in cigarette smoke as he clutched a half-empty glass of Turkish tea.

A young man who looked like his son popped outside every so

often with a fresh batch of tea. Mike and Melika could see him minding the shop through the window, cleaning and straightening the miniature carpets, clipping stray threads, sweeping. He was in constant motion. Baba Mudi appeared to holler jokes at him at regular intervals, at which the harrowed-looking young man half-smiled and shook his head.

Mike inclined his head toward the shop and looked at Melika with raised eyebrows.

"Excellent idea," she said.

Mike bowed with a flourish and offered her his arm. They headed over to the shop, eager to pick the perfect furnishing for their shared bathroom.

Baba Mudi smiled widely at them as they approached.

"Aha! Welcome, welcome. Come inside! We have many beautiful carpet to show you. Mahmoud, çay!" He shouted the last part into the shop as he led Mike and Melika inside.

"You like çay, yes?" He gestured to the tea in his hand. They smiled and nodded politely. Mahmoud hurried away behind a curtain in the back as they entered. They could hear the tinkle of tea glasses and spoons. Baba Mudi led them to a small area by the register, where a worn old bench with fabric cushions sat. He gestured to them that they should make themselves comfortable, and then he pulled a stool out from behind the counter.

"So, you like the Turkish carpet, yes?" Baba Mudi lounged on his stool as if it were a lavishly cushioned armchair.

"Which carpet?" asked Mike stupidly.

"The carpets, we love them all," said Melika quickly, nudging him.

Baba Mudi laughed loudly. "We sell no carpet here! Only little one, mat. Carpet so big, hard to take to your home, yes?" They nodded along with him. "We have small one, so easy. And all the color!" He pointed to the numerous stacks of mats along the walls.

They were busy gazing at the columns of fabric when Mahmoud appeared with a tray of tea things.

"Mahmoud! My son," said Baba Mudi with pride. Mahmoud smiled and nodded at them.

"Nice to meet you," he said as he handed them their tea. "Like my father says, we have all kinds of colors and styles here, all handmade by the two of us. They're perfect for bathrooms, kitchens, or even welcome mats. And they make a great Turkish souvenir. A traditional item, but with a twist for your travel convenience."

"Allahallah, Mahmoud, so much blah blah," Baba Mudi cut in with a slap on Mahmoud's back. "Show them the mat." Mahmoud suppressed an eye roll, nodded, and gathered several mats from around the shop. Then he set them on the floor next to Baba Mudi and held them up one by one, describing the notable features in the design and trim.

An hour and a half later, Mike and Melika were torn between a rich red one with a geometric pattern accented by birds and a softer blue one covered in flowers.

"This is Turkish tulip," said Baba Mudi, stroking one of the flowers with a hairy finger. "Very beautiful."

"You know what? Let's take it." Melika sounded exhausted. Baba Mudi clapped his hands and rang them up while Mahmoud rolled and tied their purchase for them.

It was surprisingly easy to fit the mat into their luggage. When they arrived home and unpacked, it looked flawless against the tiled floor of the bathroom.

"It's perfect," Melika said, happy despite her flight-induced exhaustion.

"Great," agreed Mike with half-closed eyes. They stumbled to their bed to sleep off their jet lag, dead to the world the minute they hit the mattress.

If they had been sleeping less soundly, one of them might have gone to the bathroom in the night to find the bath mat peeking out the window. They might have encountered it examining the little room or wriggling under the crack in the door. They might have found it flitting around the kitchen on their way to get a glass of water. But instead, Mike and Melika snored through the whole night and found the mat exactly where they had left it in the morning.

Melika grinned when she stepped out of the shower, squishing her toes into the plush fibers of the mat.

"This was such a smart purchase!" she called out to Mike, who was busy groaning sleepily as he pulled an uncooperative sweater over his head.

"Yeah, we did a great job with that," came his muffled response. "Maybe we can sort out the internet next."

She rubbed her feet around for a few more seconds before wrapping herself in her towel and leaving the room. Had she been paying attention, she would have seen the mat shuddering with distaste as she exited the bathroom.

Within a week, the house began to unravel at its seams. Open windows let in wind that blew unpaid bills into secret nooks and crannies. Rain leaked into unsealed spice jars sitting on the kitchen windowsill. Empty glasses left on the coffee table inevitably ended up shattered and glittering in the carpet. One morning, Mike walked into the kitchen to find that a large bottle of olive oil had broken and somehow spread to every corner of the room. Mousetraps snapped shut on themselves, the freezer was left ajar, and every cord in the house was mysteriously unplugged.

"That's it. Either we're crazy or there is a ghost in this house," Melika said, hands clenched at the sight of the curtain rod splayed like a fallen sword across the living room.

"Maybe we should get a dog," said Mike. "A guard dog."

"A dog would make things worse. What do you think a dog would do to these curtains?"

Mike shrugged. "How about a cat? Cats are friendly with ghosts, right?"

Snugglemuffin was a hefty black-and-white fellow with a scarred ear and a pink nose. He was a bit suspicious of the world in general but purred loudly when scratched on the rump. The shelter had assured

Mike and Melika that he would quickly settle into his new home and warm up to them.

Snugglemuffin did not settle in well at all, and Mike and Melika almost instantly regretted adopting him. He woke them in the middle of the night with earsplitting yowls, ran up and down the halls at all hours, and hissed at them whenever they came out of the bathroom. His litter was constantly sprinkled outside of the box as if some explosion had disrupted it, and it got stuck in Mike's slippers on a daily basis.

"That cat is driving me insane," said Mike from beneath a pillow one night as Snugglemuffin capered loudly outside their bedroom door.

"Why did we think a pet was a good idea?" asked Melika with a palm pressed to her forehead. Snugglemuffin let out a war cry that made them cringe. Melika sighed and reached over to the bedside table to press play on the stereo. Frank Sinatra boomed over the sound of the frantic cat outside until they were finally able to drift back into a restless sleep.

The next morning, everything became clear to the exhausted couple.

Snugglemuffin was tearing through the house, covered in mustard. Mike had been chasing him, with Melika trailing behind and wiping down yellow streaks, when Mike inadvertently barreled into a freshly-watered house plant and found himself dripping with mud. Melika threw down her cloth and escorted Mike to the shower. While he was rinsing off, she collected all the broken jars of condiments and attempted to track down Snugglemuffin, who appeared to have gone into hiding.

She didn't think to look behind the toilet.

When Mike stepped out of the shower, the bath mat made a move. It slid abruptly to the left, just as Melika popped her head in to ask Mike if he had seen Snugglemuffin. The resounding crack of Mike's arm breaking against the tiles was immediately followed by the steady hiss of a cat urinating. Melika looked over to see

Snugglemuffin's claws buried securely in the bath mat. The elegant blue tulips were steadily turning green, the background yellow.

The mat began to buck and twist as the cat soiled its hand-dyed fibers. Mike and Melika stared as it spiraled into the air, Snugglemuffin screeching madly as the mat tried to shake him off. They got tangled in the shower curtain for a moment, and Melika was wise enough to run to the window and pry it open. As cat and mat erupted from the folds of the curtain, Melika ducked.

When she stood again, Snugglemuffin was perched calmly on the windowsill and there was no sign of the mat. Mike groaned from below the hand towels.

"Did all of that really just happen?" he asked Melika, who, from the look on her face, had forgotten how to use her eyelids. She was too busy staring at their cat to reply. Snugglemuffin blinked at her and casually licked a paw. Mike's arm throbbed painfully. So painfully that he all but forgot about the mustard, the soil clogging the shower drain, and the runaway bath mat.

"Hey, Melika, remember that awful sound a minute ago? My arm is definitely broken."

Melika still didn't say a word.

"I'm dying here!" he added in a heated tone that made Snugglemuffin stop licking himself.

Melika started. "Ah, honey, I'm so sorry!" She dropped to the ground to help Mike up. After a few curse words, several sharp gasps, and more apologies, the two of them hobbled out into the hallway.

Melika glanced at the cat, who stretched out along the windowsill, turning his watchful gaze to the discolored square of carpet fluttering wildly between the trees. She doubled back to close the window with a snap, separating cat and mat indefinitely. She checked all the other windows on their way out of the house.

"Looks like rain," said Mike as Melika backed down the driveway. He was right; the clouds were heavy and morose over their little home.

A lonely whirl of blue flickered at the edge of Melika's vision, interrupting the grayness of the sky. She sighed, put the car in park, and went to take their box of good china off a shelf in the garage. She wiped a mat-sized area of the shelf clean with a rag before returning to the car without a word. Mike raised his eyebrows.

"You're leaving the garage door open for that little terror, aren't you?"

Melika scowled at him.

"You know we'll both feel guilty if we just abandon it. We brought it here in the first place."

Mike let out a strained laugh.

"I think I'm going to dig out Baba Mudi's business card when we get back," he said. "It seems we missed some information about how to care for our handcrafted Turkish rug."

They drove in silence to the hospital, wondering what on Earth they were supposed to do with a mat like that.

Merlin and the Rajin

Sir Andross Draneg

Merlin smashed through the underbrush with as much speed as his ten-year-old legs could muster. The forest air was crisp with the coming winter, the ground covered in golden-brown leaves. Above him, spindly branches reached for the sky, unconcerned with the village boy frantically seeking shelter under their bare canopy.

His hose caught and ripped as he went. The dry twigs on the ground cut into his feet, the old, rotting wooden pattens over his leather boots no longer a reliable source of protection. Despite the snags to his clothing and skin, Merlin ran. His heart slammed against his chest, and he struggled to breathe, gasping as he plowed on into the heart of Bleng Forest. He could no longer tell if the pounding he heard was from the feet of his pursuers or his own blood gushing through his veins.

The late-afternoon sun filtered down. Merlin spotted a break in the thick trees. He paused on the edge of a large meadow. Crossing would leave him exposed. Should he risk it? Voices hollered from behind him.

"Oh, Merlin!" the lordling's voice echoed through the still air. "You won't escape your punishment. You'll be a fun addition to the village square."

Merlin shuddered at the singsong intonation. An image of the large paddle Baron Gartel would use on him filled his mind. Then the look of excitement that Merlin had always noted on the baron's ruddy face when he punished the servants flashed before his eyes. The last time, Merlin had been unable to sit for two weeks.

Cackling laughter filled the forest as the baron's son and his friends pursued their prey. The baying of a hound reminded Merlin that minutes mattered.

Taking a shuddering breath, Merlin crashed into the open area and sped up. He had to make it to the other side. His feet crushed the dried, yellowed ground. He was almost there. Almost.

Pain shot through his thigh. Merlin stumbled, clutching his pierced flesh. An arrow protruded from between his fingers, warm blood oozing over his hand. He cried out but refused to go down. With his free hand, he pawed the ground and kept himself moving forward toward the safety of the trees. A second arrow whistled past his head as he bobbed, the pain nearly felling him once more.

Merlin staggered into the thick brown-orange brush and kept going. Fire raced up his injured leg with each step, but he couldn't stop. He just couldn't.

Then the ground turned rocky. His foot struck a small boulder, and he went down. The jarring impact rushed up his body, rattling his teeth. Crawling to his knees, he rose once more, stumbled, and landed on a . . . chair.

His brain registered that he was on an actual wooden chair . . . in the middle of the forest. Heart pounding, chest heaving, he glanced down at the unexpected piece of furniture. His eyes fell on the thick shaft of the arrow, and he shuddered in pain, feeling the sticky warmth of his blood sluice between his fingers.

Then he noticed the carvings on the jet-black wood of the chair's leg. The etching consisted of symbols Merlin didn't recognize. He'd spent many hours poring over books in the baron's library. Friar Tully, who'd taken a liking to him, had insisted on Merlin becoming his apprentice. He'd taught Merlin to read various languages, including Latin and the old runes that were the friar's particular passion.

But these symbols didn't form any language Merlin knew. It was certainly not Latin nor French nor even Danish. Merlin's mind brought forth the images of the Druid tribe whom Baron Gartel had run off. Their writing seemed to match. He'd picked up some of it during Friar Tully's meeting with the tribe's high priestess. Running a trembling hand over the carved symbols, he attempted to sound them out in a whisper.

A gush of wind swirled around him as he sat on the strange chair. Merlin closed his eyes, guarding them against the dirt and leaves that swished about him. Shielding his face with his hand, he risked a peek. The forest debris swirled in a circle, surrounding the spot. Bright golden light glimmered in a mist. As the chair spun, Merlin spotted Baron Gartel's son and the nobles who'd pursued him. They had entered the forest from the clearing and now stood dumbfounded. Merlin would have laughed at their snobby faces covered in shock, but he was too scared. What was happening?

The chair spun faster. The forest debris was gone. The golden glimmer turned into a soft lavender hue. Merlin forgot to hold his injured leg and gripped the chair with both hands, hoping to stay on. There was a whoosh and then a boom, and the chair stopped. Merlin's eyes took in the darkness that now prevailed around him. He shivered in the sudden cold. The chair floated in an empty void. Then a small orange dot appeared, growing rapidly larger. It became a massive ball of spiraling gas. Merlin's mouth fell open in shock at its enormity. Then it was gone.

Merlin realized the chair was actually moving at a tremendous speed. He longed to look back to see the giant ball disappear, but he dared not move lest he fall off into . . . where was he? Other balls of varying size and color grew from specks into monumentally gigantic objects, then swept past. Sparkling dots sprinkled the darkness about him in between those moments. Awe at what he beheld warred with fear of the unknown. Merlin's stomach tightened in apprehension as his journey on the chair prolonged itself.

Then the magical piece of furniture resumed its twirling, and the golden-lavender mist materialized around him once more. Then it stopped. The glowing ceased.

Merlin looked about in awestruck wonder. The chair had deposited itself in a gleaming white marble chamber. Relief flooded through him as he found himself on solid ground. It was followed by curiosity about his new surroundings. Merlin gazed about, wide-eyed, taking it all in. The room was shaped like a hexagonal rotunda and towered several feet high. The ceiling seemed to be made of the same wood as the chair, its beams curving and arching in beautiful patterns to form a pointed dome.

"Who are you?"

The musical voice brought Merlin's attention back down from the ceiling. His gaze was filled with the angelic countenance of a young girl who looked to be about his age. Her gloriously clear blue eyes looked at him with interest, and her flowing gold hair tumbled in waves almost to her feet.

"I'm Merlin." His voice sounded oddly calm, considering what he had experienced only moments ago, and his chest swelled with pride at his own courage. "Who are you?"

"I'm Vivelda," she answered. "You're wounded."

Merlin pulled his eyes away from hers, following her gaze as she took in the arrow protruding from his thigh. "It hurts a lot," Merlin heard himself say. He made a movement, as if to yank the weapon from his flesh.

Her hands slapped his away. "You'll bleed out." She knelt down beside him. Soft fingers touched his leg around the embedded arrow. "Oh Great I Am, grant me your healing power."

Warmth spread across Merlin's thigh. The pain dissolved away. A soft shimmer of golden light filled the space beneath her hands, covering his wound. Slowly, the arrow moved up and out of his body, tumbling to the marble floor. The heat and glow remained. Comfort and peace filled Merlin. He'd never experienced anything like the serenity that now encompassed him.

"There, all well," she said, rocking back on her heals and grinning at him like a content cat. "So, Merlin, what are you doing here?"

"I don't know where here is." He moved his hand over his now fully healed thigh. Even his clothing had been restored.

"You are in the great temple of Artaxyoun." Her voice filled with pride as she spoke.

"Where is that?" he asked.

Her lovely face wrinkled into a frown. "It is on the Rajin moon of Ghoukas. This is where the Rajin study and train primarily, though, of course, the local temples can train Rajin as well."

"Of course," he said, not wanting to seem like an idiot. He had no idea what she was talking about.

"Come," she said, bouncing up onto the balls of her feet. "We must go show you to Rajin LaRoo. He will clear everything up."

"Right." Merlin rose from the chair and followed her.

She led him to one of seven doors that led off the rotunda where his chair had landed. Merlin glanced around at the white marble walls and floors. Portraits of human men and women in red robes lined their path. Scattered among them, other paintings showed strange creatures in similar garments. All along the corridor were closed doors on either side. Merlin longed to glance inside the rooms they passed. His guide, however, continued forward at a brisk walk, so he followed along meekly.

Soon they arrived at a set of massive double doors made of the same jet-black wood as the chair. Without knocking or hesitating, Vivelda plowed on through them. Merlin trailed after her, amazed by the confidence revealed in the way she held her shoulders and her head. Though slight in stature, she exuded a certain powerful essence Merlin had only ever seen before in Lady Gartel. It spoke of one accustomed to commanding, and he wondered if this place was the home of a great king. Was this magical girl a princess? Perhaps a queen?

Passing into the space beyond the doors, Merlin found himself in a second rotunda. He came to a stop, looking about with curiosity. The chamber was hexagonal like the first, though this one had stairs spiraling up the sides, leading to a series of protruding platforms. Above him, a stained-glass window showered colorful light across the white marble of the floors. Gazing up at the window, Merlin took in the shape of a cross, wreathed at the top by a crown of thorns and surrounded by seven droplets of blood red.

The dome-shaped glass depiction shocked him. Friar Tully had a book with that exact picture in it. Questions swirled in his mind. How was this possible? Where was he? Who were these Rajin people? How could they heal with that strange light?

"So you are the young man who arrived on the chair," a voice, deep and gruff, startled Merlin.

He'd been so lost in thought that he hadn't noticed Vivelda continuing on without him in search of the person she'd mentioned. Now before him stood a tall, thin man in a scarlet robe. His long black hair was secured in a ponytail at his nape, and he had a matching beard that reached to well below his waist. His eyes were almond slits, and the penetrating stare he directed at Merlin made their amber color almost glow.

"Y-yes . . . sir," Merlin managed to stammer out.

"I found him in the meditation chamber, Master," Vivelda added from where she stood beside the man.

"Interesting." The man's brow furrowed, making his bushy eyebrows meet in the middle. "Come, sit with me and tell me where you are from, young sir."

He gestured for Merlin to follow and led the way to a cushioned bench at the far side of the space. There were two small sofas placed in front of the bench. The man took one, while Vivelda took the other. Merlin settled onto the soft purple cushion of the bench. Silver threads depicted constellations that Merlin could not recognize. He ran a trembling hand over it, realized there was still blood on his fingers, and withdrew it lest he stain the beautiful material.

"Ah, yes," the man said, reaching forward and taking Merlin's bloody hand. "You mentioned he was injured when you found him." A deep purple glow emanated from the man's hand as he held Merlin's. When he let go, Merlin stared at his now-clean hand.

"Yes, Master," Vivelda said. "He had an arrow in his thigh."

"An arrow." The man's brows rose in surprise, forming a bushy triangle over his almond-shaped eyes. "So tell me, young man, who are you and where do you come from?"

"My name is Merlin. I come from a small village called Gosforth, My Lord." Merlin wasn't sure if the man was a noble, but he figured it was best to address him as though he were. Watching the man settle back into the sofa and study him with those glowing amber eyes, Merlin continued. "I am apprentice to Friar Tully at Gosforth Manor, the home of Baron Gartel."

"I see." The man's face furrowed into a frown once more. "And tell me, Merlin, how came you to be traveling on a Hoshi chair?"

"The baron's son and some of his friends were teasing a young village girl. It made me mad, so I hurled some shi—ah . . . ." Merlin's cheeks reddened at his near misstep. Friar Tully would be displeased to know his apprentice had been about to use vulgar language. "I ran from them and into the forest, and there I found the chair."

"And these nobles shot you, I take it?"

"Yes, My Lord."

"Well, Merlin." The man's voice held a note of respect that Merlin found confusing. "You did well, saving the young girl from those ruffians."

"It won't be good for me when I return. They'll put me on display in the village and have everyone throw dung at me. And Baron Gartel is sure to give me a whipping." Merlin's heart deflated at the thought. It would not be the first time; he really needed to just stay out of other people's battles. Yet something compelled him to help whenever he saw injustice.

"You don't need to return." The man leaned forward, staring into Merlin's eyes. "You could stay here and study to be a Rajin."

"What is a Rajin?" Merlin asked. "Where am I?"

"Your planet is part of a larger collection of planets we call Thyrein's Galactic Wall. This is a moon that serves as the headquarters for our order. The Rajin, like your Friar Tully, follow the Great I Am and train to use His power to help others and bring knowledge to all beings in our universe."

Merlin looked from the man to the young girl. She was nodding her head vigorously. Planets? He'd traveled to a different planet? Friar Tully had explained to him that Earth was the center of the universe and that all the constellations swirled around it. The holy man had speculated that there might be other planets with human life, but he had warned Merlin that such thoughts should never be spoken before the church officials.

Now, here he was, on a different world, being offered a chance at a life far more exciting than anything his tiny village could offer. Dare he stay? There was no reason not to. Orphaned long ago, he had only Friar Tully who cared about him. Would he be shown how to heal, like the girl had done? Merlin's heart picked up its pace at the possibility of learning magic. Then a small niggle of suspicion sprouted, eroding his growing enthusiasm.

"Will I ever be able to go back?" Merlin asked.

"Of course," the Rajin master answered. "Anytime. But when you do, you will be equipped with the power of the Great I Am. Perhaps you will bring a new era to your world that way."

Merlin thought about the prophecy his mother had told him. An old Druid witch had helped birth him since the midwives had been called away to help in the difficult labor of the baroness. His mother had shared with him the words the woman had spoken over him.

"She looked at you, my son," his mother's voice filled his mind now, "and she said you would be the one to bring order out of chaos. You would crown a king who would usher in a golden age."

Looking into the Rajin's eyes, Merlin made his choice.

"I'll stay and learn, if you'll have me."

The man stood. He placed both hands upon Merlin's head, and closed his eyes. Merlin could see that beneath the scarlet robe he wore a simple shirt and pants, both in a deep royal purple hue. He wondered why this man wore one color while the girl dressed in another. Did the different clothes mean anything?

Then a comforting warmth filled his body. Peace settled on him. He closed his eyes, unsure what the Rajin was doing, but unwilling to have him stop. In his mind's eye, a sword appeared. It was stuck in a great rock shaped almost like an anvil. A crown hung from the hilt.

The man lifted his hands and sat back in his chair. Merlin opened his eyes, sad that the beautiful feeling was dissipating. The man's eyes looked upon him with an odd expression Merlin couldn't place, yet it inspired in him confidence and ease. Whatever the Rajin were, they felt right . . . like Friar Tully.

"You will be the catalyst for many things, both on your world and in many others, young Merlin."

The three sat in silence for a moment. Then the Rajin turned to Vivelda and slapped his hands upon his knees. "Come then. We will get you settled in, and Lady Vivelda can show you around. You will help him, won't you, my dear?"

Vivelda turned shining blue eyes upon Merlin. "Of course, Master LaRoo. We are going to get on very well." A bright smile wreathed her face, and Merlin found it hard to breathe.

Rajin LaRoo smiled at Merlin. "I'm sure you will."

Don't Touch the Bloodbuds

Taylor Adel

Mama never did tell us what, exactly, the Bloodbuds did to people. She always just called those who touched them "infected."

We knew she thought the Bloodbuds grew at the edge of our property, bubblin' up from the dirt to choke out the bluebonnets and Indian blankets that bloomed there. She would say they liked it under them trees, what with the moss hangin' off their branches like ragged shrouds, turned to wrigglin' ghosts in the twilight hours. Mama said they didn't like the sun, them Bloodbuds. She done told us it turned them to ash, so they had to stay in the shade where they couldn't never be touch by warmth and golden sky light.

I think maybe Mama thought she knew what she was talkin' 'bout but didn't know that she really had no clue.

When Mama wasn't raisin' nonsense in the house, she was knittin'. She knitted the most beautiful things that I ever did see. One day, she gave me periwinkle socks with little rose blooms on them, and they kept my feet all nice and cozy and free of blisters. I was the only girl of her and Paw's seven kids, so I was the only one to get those little rosebuds. She made the others socks as well, with extra paddin' in the toes and at the heel so their boots wouldn't chafe 'em while they was out plowin' and harvestin' and maintainin' the farm.

Every mornin' when the boys went out with Paw, Mama would pat their backs and kiss their cheeks, and then she'd give 'em the same warnin'. She'd look 'em in the eye and go, "Don't touch them Bloodbuds, my boys. If you see 'em, with petals gray as ash and leaves the color of the settin' sun, you just run. Don't you never touch them Bloodbuds, you hear?" And she'd pin them each with her burnt brown gaze and furrowed brows. Benny and Fendrickson and Grayson and Matthew and Johnathon and Kevin would nod and say their "yes'ms" and leave out the door into the dark mornin', soon to be filled with light as they wandered to the fields. Mama would get off to her cleanin' and knittin' and cookin', and I'd get on off to the coops to take care of the hens and throw feed at the rooster.

Mama would sometimes knit us mittens. I didn't never need no mittens—it didn't get cold enough where we lived—but she made them nonetheless. She put tiny little leaves on mine, around the wrists and on the pad of each finger. The boys and Paw got 'em too, but they didn't get no nice leaves like I did. Mama started checkin' that the boys had them when they went out to work in the blazin' heat, demandin' they store the mittens in their pockets.

Matthew lost his once, and Mama wouldn't let him inside. She grabbed fistfuls of dried sage and lavender from the herb rack and threw the skeletons of the plants at him. She crunched 'em all up in her tiny hands and scattered 'em over his head like dust, screamin' that he'd touched a Bloodbud. She shrieked and cried and kept him from steppin' foot inside 'til Paw convinced her to take a spoonful of her medicine.

It was her special medicine, Paw would say as he held Mama's hand and pushed the utensil between her quiverin' bleached lips. Sometimes, he'd look at me while he gave it to her, squintin' his eyes in suspicion, like maybe I had somethin' to do with Mama needin' it. I'd just look back at him 'cause I didn't know what else to do but look at him as he looked at me.

Mama didn't never get right in her head after Matthew forgot his mittens. She'd sit all day in her rocker with a fire goin' in the hearth, sweat pourin' from her face and down her arms. Sometimes her hands would get so slick that she couldn't hold her needles no more, so I'd have to pat her down with rags and dry the needles off. She knit petite mittens for me, with vines wrappin' 'round them in the most delicate, pretty way I ever did see. I kept them tucked in my pockets and would rub the soft wool every now and again while doin' my chores. After Mama got sick—sick in her head, Paw would say—I had to do all the cleanin' and cookin'. I'd be in the kitchen makin' supper and listenin' to Mama mutter 'bout the Bloodbuds, her gaze on the fire.

She liked that fire, even though it turned the house into a furnace, and I'd have to walk out toward the fields to catch a fresh breeze beneath the blisterin' heat of the summertime sun. I couldn't put that fire out, though. No one could. Mama said that anyone infected by the Bloodbud couldn't get nowhere near a fire. She said it kept us safe. After Matthew forgot his mittens that one day, he'd warmed his hands near it to convince Mama he wasn't infected, and her face shone with relief as sweet as honey while sweat dripped down Matthew's neck and across his back from our burnin' home.

Mama said lots of things 'bout those infected with the Bloodbud. She said that they couldn't come into someone's home 'less they was invited, and that's what kept us safe—our home. She told me they didn't like to be alone, them infected ones; they'd ask others to touch the Bloodbud, and since they was so very charmin' and attractive, most people would do as they was told.

Sometimes Mama looked at me like Paw did, but less suspicious and more observant, like she was waitin' for me to say somethin' to her. She'd pat my wrist and ask to see my mittens, so I'd pull them out and let her touch them with her sandpaper hands.

A few months after Mama got sick in her head, Benny got sick in his skin. Paw said he'd caught fever. Him and my brothers stayed away while Mama and I took care of Benny. We brought him water for the heat, ginger for the rumblin' in his belly, and meadowsweet and yarrow to rid him of the illness. I tried to get Mama to put the fire out since it just made Benny worse, but she wouldn't hear nothin' of it. I was fretful that I might catch Benny's fever—his eyes was red and puffy and his skin flamin' to the touch despite his insistence of a chill—but

Mama said I didn't need to worry 'bout gettin' sick. She said her and I was safe and sound at Benny's side, so I stayed.

I never did tell no one, but Benny was my favorite brother. He treated me kind and snuck me sips of whiskey with mint leaves when Paw wasn't lookin'. Benny had wheat hair like me and eyes the color of grass like Paw and the body of a sinewy dogwood like all us kids. Yeah, Benny was like all of us save for his smile. It was infectious.

That was Benny's own special thing that he owned and no one else had. When Benny smiled, everyone smiled 'cause there wasn't nothin' else to do but smile. It flared down through his whole body and brightened his cheeks and lit up his eyes like the shimmerin' backs of beetles. Even while he was sick, Benny'd smile up at me and ask me to mix the herbs with whiskey instead of water. Sometimes I did, when Mama was busy starin' at the fire and everyone else was away for the day, tillin' the land. He'd give me a little wink and pinch my arm and charm me with that full-faced smile, and I'd grin back and shuffle into the rooms to fix the boys' beds. Yeah, Benny was my favorite.

I was a bit sad when Benny got better, I'm 'shamed to say. He left to go back to the fields, and I was alone with Mama and her mutterin' again. One day, she made me sit on the floor in front of the hearth while she rocked in her chair, the knittin' needles restin' in her lap. In a pile beside her, she had pairs upon pairs of mittens in sizes for all of us. She rocked and rocked in her chair, the pine squeakin', and watched me. The fire was broilin'; I felt like I was meltin' in my own skin, like the water in my body might be boilin' in the same way I'd make the stew do for supper.

Mama reached down and brushed my hair back, pullin' wet strands off my neck. I looked up at her, my eyes mirrors of her own, and tried not to groan when she asked "Did I ever tell you 'bout the Bloodbuds?" as though I had never heard of the Bloodbuds. I tried to hide the slump of my shoulders.

"Did Paw give you your medicine, Mama?" I asked 'stead of answerin' her. She just watched me and tilted her head.

"It don't work no more, not that it ever did work right 'fore. It helps the thoughts, though, you'll see. You'll need it too, one day.

You'll have too many thoughts, and you'll start seein' too many things at once, and then you'll need the medicine to get things all settled down right in your head."

I didn't like that. Why did Mama tell me I'd need the medicine too? I pulled her hand away from my hair and patted it affectionately, the skin pruned from her time near the hearth. Standin', I told her I needed to get some air and was goin' down to the creek to finish the laundry before sunset. She gripped my wrist hard, yankin' me toward her. Eyes large, like a fly's in its beady body, she reached into my pocket and felt for the mittens. Certain they was there, she released me, and I startled away from her. She didn't notice nothin', only sayin', "Okay, Lilly, I'll be here."

That was a strange day, and I never did look at Mama the same after that. Whatever was wrong in her head, it was gettin' worse. When I told Paw, his frown cast a shadow down the length of his whitenin' beard before he headed inside to get her medicine. Mama started takin' it in the mornin' and at night after that. Paw continued to watch me like I might be a rattler in disguise, and Mama would ask me to sit with her so she could talk to me 'bout the Bloodbuds she'd created in her mind. She told me the Bloodbud grew year-round and that it couldn't be scattered by bees or butterflies or other bugs, the way some plants could. She told me it only grew in the shadows where someone had been killed. She insisted it blossomed from the blood of the fallen, and the roots feasted on the corpse as they grew.

Mama started makin' me nervous. The more she talked 'bout the Bloodbuds, the more I feared for her head and got frightened of sittin' near her in front of the hearth. One evenin' after supper, I asked Benny to go to the spring with me for water, seein' as it was after dark and all. He carried the jugs, and I tottered beside him with a lantern, the oil burnin' bright under the moonless sky. I told him 'bout Mama and the Bloodbuds and her medicine. I even told him 'bout the funny things she said to me and the strange way Paw would look at me sometimes. He didn't joke or tell me I was gettin' stuffy, shut up in the house all day with the crazy swarmin' 'round me. He filled the water jugs and told me he'd put the Bloodbud talk to rest for good. I smiled at him and he smiled at me, and even with the lamp givin' off the only light, I saw it was the kind of smile that belonged to Benny, and Benny alone. We went back to the house and that was that.

The day after I told Benny that Mama was gettin' worse, it had been exactly one year since she'd fallen ill. The pile of mittens beside her had grown to a tower, and she didn't know I'd pull some from the bottom every night after she and Paw went to bed and toss them in the fire to burn. I didn't tell her that sometimes I thought the fire made shapes. Shapes of rose petals and leaves and vines—always yellow and orange and red. Things like that happen when looking at a fire for too long. Little white dots appear on the backs of my eyelids after lookin' at the fire, same as when I'd look at the sun, so seein' things in the fire isn't all that different from seein' things when lookin' away. That's what I'd tell myself when I saw them shapes.

I didn't tell nobody else 'bout Mama. No one but Benny. Benny said he'd do somethin' to end the talk 'bout the Bloodbuds, and he wouldn't make no lies 'bout somethin' like that. He started leavin' his mittens in the chicken coop too. He said they got in the way as he was workin' and asked me to stay quiet 'bout it. I said yes, thinkin' there wasn't no sense in the mittens, anyway.

I waited and waited for one week, hopin' he knew how he was goin' to help Mama understand that there wasn't no Bloodbuds on our property and that she didn't need to worry 'bout them ever again.

It was hot the day Benny came back to the house in the middle of his work, when he should have been helpin' Kevin out in the field. I was makin' the beds and Mama was sittin' in her chair knittin' when he knocked on the door. We was expectin' Mrs. Fletching and her bags of flour, so I caught surprise at seein' Benny in the doorway, his hands stuffed in his pockets. Green-grass eyes crossed over me, and he peered into the house.

"What's Ma doin, Sissy?" he asked, watchin' over my shoulder.

Wipin' my hands off on my dress, I leaned around the wall to find her rockin' beside the hearth, her lips flashin' teeth as she muttered to herself.

"Same thing she always doin'—sittin' in her rocker, talkin'

nonsense 'bout nonsense. What you doin' here, Benny? Paw's gon' grip off your ear for shirkin' chores."

Benny leaned back, glancin' around. "What's Ma mutterin' 'bout?"

Brows furrowed at his bizarre behavior, I shook my head.

"Who's to say?" I threw my hands up at him. "Benny, really now, what you doin' here? Get on back to work, and I'm gonna get on back to fixin' your bedsheets. Go, get on."

He frowned at me, his cheeks flattenin' in aggravation.

"I gotta come in for just one second and talk to Ma, Sissy. You gonna let me in so I can talk to Ma?"

I stepped aside. I was ready to tell Benny to hurry on up, when Benny smiled at me. It wasn't a Benny smile, though. This one ended at his lips and never reached his eyes, leavin' his cheeks undimpled before simmerin' out soon after it came. It didn't charm me at all the way I was used to bein' charmed into givin' Benny his way. I didn't have the urge to grin on back. No, this wasn't a Benny smile at all.

"What you wanna talk to Mama 'bout?" I asked, shovin' my hands in my own pockets and graspin' the mittens with the vines woven 'round them, so delicate and pretty.

"I just wanna talk to her 'bout the Bloodbuds. 'Member, you asked me to find out 'bout the Bloodbuds?"

"Yeah, I 'member," I said, takin' another step away from him. "But I don't think you should be botherin' Mama with that. I think we should just leave her to her thoughts. There's no reason to be botherin' her 'bout the thoughts she has, even if they is crazy."

Benny's smile slipped away, and his face darkened as he gripped the doorframe.

"Let me in now, Lillian," he growled at me, his gaze puncturin' mine.

I didn't know what I should do—he seemed so angry—when a voice behind me cried out, "Lilly, away from that door!" I stumbled back as Mama flung a fistful of herb dust at Benny.

Her face was flushed, and sweat dripped down her body from her time by the hearth. The mist settled over Benny, and he howled like I'd heard coyotes do at night while they was huntin'. The sound filled my ears, and I flinched from the noise, listenin' as it turned from screams to laughter. Benny was bent over in hysteria, his eyes bright with amusement at Mama's shock, 'fore he lunged at the exposed threshold. As he was 'bout to cross over, Benny pulled up short and beat the outside of the frame, his mouth foamin', and Mama dragged me away from him. She dropped what was left of the herbs on the floor to keep hold of me. Benny peered at us.

"Silly little medicine woman. Silly little witch. You don't know nothin' 'bout the Bloodbud. I can't get you and your little girl, but your boys is out here. I'll just wait for them. How's that sound, Ma?"

Benny grinned at me with a sneer and raised his brows.

"Wanna see the Bloodbuds, Lilly? They all nice and pretty. I think you'd like 'em, same as I did."

I blinked at him. *Do I wanna see the Bloodbuds? They do seem like they'd be worth looking for, the way he says it.*

Mama wrapped an arm 'round my waist, and I done shook my head. *No, I won't go nowhere with him.* Benny shrugged as he sauntered away from where we was huddled together inside the doorway.

"I thought she was like you, with those eyes all willow moss and kindlin'. No matter. Shut your door and sleep well, Ma."

Mama did as Benny said and pulled me to the floor with her as she fell into her tears and wails. All night we sat, waitin' for my brothers and Paw, until finally we fell asleep together on the wood in front of the doorway. When we woke that next mornin', there wasn't a sound to be heard. Mama tucked me up against the wall and opened the door. Slow as a caterpillar makin' its way across a branch, the door slid inward to reveal the outside beyond. Mama's grip went white, and I screamed into hands that shook with such violence I couldn't feel them no more.

Bodies lay in a trail to the trees, each of my brothers settled face up in front of us. I knocked them off, one by one, in the mornin' light: Matthew, Johnathon, Kevin, Fendrickson, and Grayson. Moanin', I crawled to the threshold, only to be stopped by Mama's strong hand at the nape of my neck.

My eyes traced the line of my family members to the trees, where the last body was left discarded. Paw's face stared up, watchin' with blank eyes for the sun to appear and break the darkness of his restin' place beneath the willows. His beard was the color of rust, as was his chest and his hands and the ground around him. My eyes gripped him, flailed over him, and rested with a harsh finality on a little spot above his chest. There, the blooms was gray, gray like a thundercloud, and the adolescent leaves was all russet and bold.

A Bloodbud.

When a Dragon Sings

Citlalin Ossio

Victory sat with the choir in the church hall. The light shining through the stained-glass windows painted a kaleidoscope of colors on the singers' faces as they finished the offertory hymn. Victory noticed a young man, a few years older than her, fixing his copper-rimmed glasses on his nose for the eighth time. His off-white coat would've matched the priest's had the Church's crest been sewn on the sleeves.

Father Isaac began the thanksgiving ceremony, and the congregation knelt to pay respect. As he raised a glistening golden chalice, a dragon's roar interrupted him and echoed in the church through the open doors. He and everyone else stared out the colorful windows in disbelief. The dragon didn't sound close enough to cause an immediate panic, but the startled churchgoers whispered with wonder even as the service ended, and they exited into the bright morning light.

Victory made her way through the garden to the church's adjacent residence building and enjoyed the cooling breeze on her bare arms. A few loose strands of her dark brown hair floated in the air. She pushed the dragon from her mind and went to work, but after a few hours of its occasional roars, it became too distracting to ignore. Even though she didn't understand what it was saying, she knew it was in pain.

She played with her ragged crystal necklace as she walked down the same hall she had walked a million times in the past fifteen years since arriving at St. Francis when she was five. The serene sound of the fountains contrasted with the occasional roars that echoed through the air. Victory wished she could understand what the poor creature was saying, but her dragon ancestry only provided her with fire, which she could only control with the gem that hung around her neck.

"Father Isaac, may I speak with you?" she asked, peeking into his office,

"Come in, Victory. I was just about to send for you." He motioned her forward with his usual warm smile.

Father Kiyoshi sat across from him. His stern expression was grimmer than usual as he stared down at his clasped hands, deep in thought.

"Good afternoon, Father Kiyoshi. Oh!" Victory was surprised to see the young man from the morning service with them. He fixed his coat collar, as he had a few times in church.

"Ah, this is Camilo," introduced Father Isaac. "He's studying for the priesthood and will be finishing his training here in Seria Longpointe. This is Victory, my favorite child." He smiled proudly.

"This is some way to treat your favorite child," said Father Kiyoshi indignantly.

Camilo stretched out his hand. "It's nice to meet you, Victory." His voice had a gentle ring.

She returned the greeting, but his unexpected presence made her hold her breath. She glanced uncertainly at Father Isaac.

"It's okay," he said. "I assume you're here about the dragon?"

She nodded, knowing now it was safe to proceed. "I think it's hurt."

Father Isaac nodded. "Father Kiyoshi and I believe so as well."

"We think it could be trapped somewhere in the mountains near Wake Zost, perhaps from a rock slide," Father Kiyoshi said. He looked at his fellow priest with concerned eyes. "And he wants you two to go save the creature."

"What?" Victory and Camilo asked in shocked unison.

Camilo fixed his glasses. "I'm just a seminarian. What could I do?"

"You're the best healer we have," said Father Isaac.

"But I don't know anything about dragons."

"That's why Victory will go with you." Father Isaac locked eyes with her. She swallowed hard and fiddled with her stone necklace. "She's part dragon by descent and will be able to communicate with the beast."

"B-but I don't understand it," she stuttered. "I can't even control my fire without this." She raised her necklace.

"Fire?" Camilo raised a brow, but he was ignored.

"I think it's too dangerous," grumbled Father Kiyoshi.

Father Isaac walked up to Victory and held her shoulders. "You can do this, Victory. You'll do very well. Have faith."

She looked up at the man who had raised her and would get her and the other orphans out of trouble when Father Kiyoshi caught them misbehaving and causing mischief. She trusted him above anyone else, and his trust in her gave her courage.

She took a deep breath. "I'll do my best."

He smiled warmly and proudly, then turned to Camilo. "Well, Camilo?"

He let out a sigh, then smiled weakly. "What's the plan?"

"Excellent!" Father Isaac walked to a bookshelf in the corner of the room as Father Kiyoshi sighed and shook his head. "You'll need to leave as soon as possible. As you know, dragons are extremely rare. Once people realize it's trapped, they'll want to capture it and sell it, or worse." He unrolled a weathered map on top of his desk and pointed to the mountains he believed the dragon was stuck in.

"Do you have evenroot here?" asked Camilo.

"No, you'll have to find some on your way."

"Where's the nearest waterfall?"

"There's one about a quarter of the way there," answered Father Kiyoshi. "It's small, but you should find the plant there." He paused. "Just make sure you stay safe."

Once they mapped out the quickest route, they left the office and each prepared for the trip. Victory holstered her trusty mint-gold slingshot and stored seeds tipped with different colors in bags sewn onto her belt, while Camilo packed a variety of plants and extracts.

Before leaving, they stopped by the chapel to light candles for a safe journey and then made their way to the west gate. As they exited the city, another pained roar rang through the air.

They followed the main road that cut through the forest. By late afternoon, they reached a small clearing through which a river ran, and they saw the small cataract Father Kiyoshi had mentioned.

"So what does evenroot look like?" Victory asked as she stepped into the fresh, clear water. She followed Camilo as he trekked closer to the cascade. Water splashed and soaked them.

"It's a black-and-white root," he answered. "It'll be growing from the underside of a rock."

Her jaw dropped as she took in the abundance of stones around her. "You mean we have to look under every rock?" She bent down and scooped up a few with both hands. None had an evenroot growing from them.

"Try the bigger ones with jagged edges." He picked up a stone matching the description. "Like this one." He dropped it back into the water with a soft plop.

After a short while, Victory found a white root attached to a rock. She excitedly revealed her finding. "Camilo, Camilo! I found it!" She splashed water everywhere as she ran to her companion's side to show off her treasure.

Camilo took one look at it and chuckled softly. "Sorry to disappoint you, but that root hasn't matured enough. It's missing the black."

"Oh." Victory's shoulders slumped, and she dropped her red herring back into the river. She got on her knees to continue searching, and the water reached up to her elbows. Glancing behind her to make sure Camilo wasn't looking, she lifted her pink undershirt just enough to reveal the side of her stomach, where a patchy area of dark forest green stood out against her light-olive skin. The running water felt cool and refreshing on her skin and scales.

"When did you find out you were part dragon?"

She flinched and turned to see Camilo searching next to her. She quickly pulled down her undershirt. *Did he see them?* she wondered. She moved a little farther away from him.

"After Father Isaac found me. I don't remember much, but before I went to St. Francis, I grew up out here, in the wild. When I saw other people like me, I thought we were all the same, but a few years later I learned . . ." She picked up a ragged rock that stood out among a pile of smooth ones. "That there was something wrong with me."

"Nothing's wrong with you."

Victory looked up and locked eyes with Camilo. She hadn't noticed before how, behind his glasses, his golden eyes stood out against his dark-olive skin. They were warm.

"Have you noticed that most of the rocks here are smooth?" he asked as he continued searching.

"Yeah," Victory answered with a raised brow.

"But the ones we're looking for are different. They're rough and may seem out of place." He walked toward Victory with his hands behind his back. "But because they're not like the rest, they're the most special." He stopped in front of her and bent down. "Because they hold something great." He put his hand out and turned it over to reveal a rock with a fully matured evenroot growing on it.

Victory gasped with excitement, and her eyes widened. "Wow!"

Camilo chuckled and handed her the rock. She stared at the white roots that transitioned into black at the bottom.

"Now we just need to find two more like this one."

They continued their search, but his words played through Victory's head. "Camilo, aren't you afraid of me?"

"I have no reason to be," he said matter-of-factly.

"I'm part dragon. I have scales across my body. I breathe *fire*."

"But you've never purposefully hurt anyone, right?"

She nodded.

Camilo sighed regretfully and stared at his hands through the water. "I used to steal from people, hardworking people." He lowered his voice. "I did hurt people." After a while, he turned and smiled warmly at his companion. "I'm not afraid of you, Victory."

She heard the sincerity in his voice and was relieved. Suddenly, another roar echoed through the forest.

"What I am afraid of is not reaching the dragon in time. It seems to be getting impatient."

Victory turned over a rock and grew excited when she found an evenroot there. Minutes later, she found a second one. "I won," she joked, holding up two fingers in a victory sign.

They ate a snack while drying off and were set to continue their journey when a scream from the woods startled them. Their worried expressions mirrored each other. Suddenly, a light-haired young man, maybe three years younger than Victory, burst out of the forest, booking it as fast as he could toward them.

"Ahhh! Help!" he screamed. His huge duffel bag clanked and rattled as he ran. Then a floating pink light emerged from the trees behind him. Even though the sun was shining, it was shadowless.

"Great," muttered Victory, readying her slingshot.

"It's just a forest fairy," said Camilo, confused.

"It's not a fairy, and it's not just one." As she spoke, four more floating lights of different colors emerged from the forest. She ran toward the screaming boy and the floating lights.

"Wait, Victory!"

As she neared the boy, she told him to go with Camilo. Then she aimed her slingshot and fired a gold-tipped seed at the pink light in front. It whimpered before charging at her. Victory rolled forward to dodge it and shot once more, this time only grazing it.

As the pink monster flew toward her, it opened its mouth wide and spit out a white venom that Victory barely avoided. The venom landed on the ground and burned the grass to a brown patch. The monster turned and dashed toward Victory, and just as it reached her, she shot a red-tipped seed into its mouth. The light swallowed it, and its white eyes widened with regret before it exploded in a cloud of pink smoke and glitter.

Victory turned and aimed at the other four lights, but they cried fearfully and dashed back into the forest. She stood up and brushed herself off before heading back to the guys.

"Whoa!" The stranger clapped enthusiastically as she neared. "That was incredible!"

"What were they?" asked Camilo.

Victory holstered her slingshot. "They're pavirils. They disguise themselves as the friendly forest fairies to lure their prey. Then they attack with their paralyzing venom."

"It fooled me." The young man put a hand over his heart and breathed a sigh of relief.

"You can tell them apart by their shadow, or lack thereof," said Victory. "Forest fairies have a shadow, but pavirils don't."

"How did you know there was more than one?" asked Camilo.

"Nothing usually travels alone in the woods, especially so close to night." She turned to the young man. "Are you okay?"

"I'm still in one piece, thanks to you." He stretched out his hand and smiled brightly. "The name's Ontriovan, but you can call me Ontri." He turned to Camilo and shook his hand.

"I'm Camilo."

Victory took Ontri's outstretched hand next. "I'm Victory."

"Where you guys headed?"

Camilo shared a glance with Victory before answering. "We're on our way toward Wake Zost to deliver medicines."

It's not a complete lie, thought Victory.

"Wake Zost?" Ontri's face lit up. "I'm headed there too. Do you guys mind if I tag along?"

"Uh . . ." They looked at each other, unsure of what excuse to give.

He noticed their hesitation. "Look, I may not be a great fighter, but I'm a great cook! My meals can cure a weathered soul and have them up and running in no time—well, figuratively speaking. I'd be grateful for the company and protection." He accompanied his plea to join them with a bright smile.

Victory knew taking the detour to Wake Zost would put the dragon at risk, but she also knew they couldn't leave Ontri to fend for himself in the dangerous and unfamiliar woods. At least, not at night.

"We can stay together until tomorrow morning," she said. "We have to make a detour before Wake Zost, and we don't want to hold you back. Wake Zost will only be a few more hours' journey and the main road is pretty safe and calm during the day, so you'll be free of danger after we part ways."

"Sounds good to me! Anything to see the next sunrise." Ontri smiled and gave a thumbs-up.

She returned his smile, happy that they could help. She looked at Camilo, who gave her a reassuring nod. Then she noticed the sun hanging low in the sky.

"There's not many hours of daylight left," she said, clenching her fists. "Let's hurry and make as much progress as we can while there's still light, then find a vacant cave or at least an open space with a good vantage point to rest until morning." As if to emphasize their urgency, the dragon roared again, and Victory realized it was growing weaker.

Ontri flinched at the sound. "W-was that a dragon?" He whispered the last word out of fear and disbelief.

"It sounds like it's in the mountains. I'm sure we're safe here," assured Camilo with a calm smile. "Let's go."

They made their way back to the main road and continued their journey until nearly nightfall, when they stopped by a river and decided to camp on a small cliff overlooking it. The sun now shone a thin orange veil over them.

"You guys stay here while I get firewood," said Victory.

Camilo offered to go with her, but when Ontri said he would tag along, so as not to stay alone, Victory decided to go on her own. It'd be easier to fight off an enemy if she didn't have to worry about protecting them as well.

The sun was setting fast as she searched for firewood in the forest. Her eyes shifted around her as the shadows grew darker and stretched farther. She held onto her stone necklace as the cloudy memories of her lost days before the safety of the church trickled in. She remembered spending nights cowering under brush and in any crevices she could find to hide from the predators. Her only safe havens in those days had been caves or small groups of woodland creatures that would allow her to stay close.

She shook the memories out of her head and focused on her present task. The snap of a twig made her heart skip a beat, and she grabbed her slingshot, whipping her body back and forth. She was startled when a crow that nearly blended into the darkened forest flew out of the tree next to her, and she shot at the air impulsively. She breathed a relieved sigh.

"Victory, get your head together," she chided herself. *Nothing bad is going to happen.* She continued to comfort herself as she quickly searched for wood and disregarded any suspicious or frightening noise as her mind playing tricks on her.

After what felt like an eternity, she met back up with her companions, and they made a fire. Ontri proved his culinary talent with a hearty stew, even with their limited ingredients.

"This is amazing, Ontri," Camilo said as he took a bite. "Are you a chef?"

"Ha, ha, thanks!" He laughed happily. "But no, I'm just a metal merchant. Though it is my dream to open up my own place. It's a great feeling to see people enjoying the food I make, and it's an even better feeling to eat with others. I don't get to do it much, so this is a lot of fun!"

"Your family is blessed to get to eat such delicious food regularly," said Victory.

Ontri's expression darkened. "My family . . ." He let out a sad laugh. "My family thinks cooking, especially for others, is disgraceful. They're part of a guild in Crescent City. Fortune is all they care about now. I'd leave that cold world if I were braver." He smiled weakly.

After a while, Camilo spoke. "With just this simple soup, I feel restored, refreshed. Don't you, Victory?"

She smiled and nodded.

His gold eyes met Ontri's solemn green ones. "You have a gift for curing people, for healing weary souls with good food. I can't think of an easier way to reach people's hearts. I hope you won't give up on your dream that easily."

A lump caught in Ontri's throat, and though he blinked hard to prevent tears from escaping, one trailed down his cheek. "Thanks, guys." His smile had returned.

They smiled warmly at him and enjoyed their meal even more, knowing how much care Ontri had put into it.

Victory looked at Camilo and admired the healing talents he had shown with just his simple words of comfort. He was going to be an excellent priest.

They decided to take watch in turns, and Camilo volunteered first watch. Ontri happily accepted, but Victory was less eager to rest her head outside, where wild animals and monsters lurked in the darkness. When Camilo yawned, she took a chance.

"You're tired, Camilo. You sleep, and I'll be first lookout."

Camilo stifled a breath. "N-no. Go ahead and sleep. I'm not ti—" Another yawn escaped him.

"Yes, you are. I won't be able to sleep anyway, so it's okay," she urged.

Camilo remained silent and stared at the crackling fire.

"What's wrong?"

He let out a long sigh and rubbed his neck. "The truth is, I don't want to get my coat dirty," he whispered.

Victory stifled her laugh. Ontri had quickly fallen asleep and was snoring quietly next to them.

"It's stupid, I know." His blush wasn't as noticeable in the darkness.

"No, no. It's cute."

"That's even more embarrassing."

"Sorry," Victory said, holding in another giggle. She thought for a moment, then crawled closer to Camilo and turned her back to him. "You can lean on me." She patted her back.

"Uh, no. Thanks."

"Don't worry, I didn't lay on my back." She turned and gave him a reassuring smile. "It's clean."

"Mm . . ." He thought for a moment. "Okay." He turned around and leaned his back against hers. She felt his head on hers. "Am I hurting you?"

"Nope." She was careful not to shake her head as she answered.

"Thanks, Victory," he said. "You're a good person."

She smiled and then joked, "I have to be nice to a future priest."

They both chuckled quietly so as not to wake Ontri, but even when the dragon roared again, he just shifted slightly and didn't wake up.

After a few minutes, Victory heard Camilo's breathing even out, and she realized he had fallen asleep. She looked toward the night sky, where stars twinkled from behind gray smoky clouds. Then she stared at the forest in front of her and remembered the cold and lonely nights she had spent as a child in the woods and was surprised to feel so safe. Being close to someone she trusted by a warm fire, she found that, for the first time in her life, she wasn't afraid of the dark and scary things that lurked in the forest. She relaxed from the long and tiring day, and before she knew it, she had drifted off to sleep.

A young Victory, about five years old, huddled against a rock, crying. She shivered in the cold, dark woods. Scrapes ran along her arms and legs, and her small hands were covered in dirt. She wished for a safe and warm place to sleep. Suddenly, she heard a sound she had never heard before. The volume and unfamiliarity of it frightened her, until she realized she understood it.

The dragon roared again, waking Victory up. She blinked in confusion and realized with surprise that she had fallen asleep. She chuckled quietly to herself, amazed. But her happiness was short-lived as she heard rustling from the forest. Her breath caught in her throat, but nothing emerged from the trees. She released her breath, then noticed Ontri was gone.

"Camilo, wake up," she said, tapping his shoulder.

He blinked and rubbed his eyes with his coat sleeve. "Yeah, I'm awake." He yawned and stretched his arms.

"Ontri's gone."

"What?" He shot up and looked around but saw no one. "His bag is still here. Where could he have gone?"

Victory kicked dirt onto the fire. Dark smoke swirled into the even darker sky. "Let's look for him."

Camilo struggled with Ontri's bag as they searched the woods. "What's he carrying, bricks?"

A sudden rustle from the bushes made them hold their breaths. They were now deep in the forest, where monsters hunted without prejudice. Victory readied her slingshot and prayed for it to be nothing more than a run-of-the-mill, harmless woodland creature.

To their relief, Ontri tumbled out of the bushes. Leaves stuck out of his ruffled hair, and his eyes welled up. "Guys!" he cried. "I'm so happy to see you."

"Where were you?" asked Victory, putting away her slingshot. They bent down next to his slumped figure.

"N-nature called." He sniffed. "Then I saw this trail of glowing blue mushrooms, and I thought I'd pick them to cook with, but then I noticed . . ." Tears trickled down his face. "I was lost."

Victory put her hand on his shoulder, and Ontri looked up at her. "It's okay." She smiled. "We're together again. You're safe."

He sniffed. "Thanks for coming to look for me."

Camilo smiled warmly. Then he noticed a blue glow coming from the bushes. "These are the mushrooms you found?" He scooped them up in his hands and showed them to Ontri.

"Yeah," he said, wiping his tears. "They don't taste that great by themselves, but I bet they'll taste good in a soup."

Camilo hummed thoughtfully.

"Let's go back," said Victory.

Camilo handed Ontri the fluorescent mushrooms. "Thanks," he said and dropped them into his bag.

To Camilo's surprise, Ontri strapped the bag on with minimal struggle. He rubbed his shoulder and was about to ask Ontri what he was carrying when a low growl interrupted him.

They huddled together and whipped their heads back and forth as a small pack of wolves emerged from the trees, surrounding them.

"Oh, no," whispered Ontri.

"Please tell me you have a plan," Camilo whispered to Victory.

The wolves growled softly, and some bared their sharp teeth as they paced around them.

Victory swallowed hard and sweat trickled down her neck. Of all the creatures in the forest, predators like these were what she feared most. But Camilo and Ontri, and the injured dragon, were depending on her. She picked a few white-tipped seeds from her utility belt.

"When I say so, run," she whispered to her companions. She swiftly shot at the wolf in front of her, and it fell forward, whimpering, providing an opening. "Now!" she screamed. The seed had been dipped in paralyzing venom, so the wolf couldn't move.

They ran for it while the other wolves grunted in confusion and hesitated. But the leader chased after them, so the rest followed.

Victory continued to shoot back at them with white-tipped seeds and was able to stun the wolves, but it would only be temporary. They arrived back at the small cliff where they had slept, but with no bridges to cross, they were trapped.

"Let's jump," said Ontri, ready to dive into the water.

Victory hesitated.

The dragon roared tiredly.

She held Ontri back. "No, we can't. We have to save the dragon, and if we go into the water, we'll be carried to who knows where."

"What?" Ontri scrunched his eyebrows together.

"That dragon is stuck in the mountains," clarified Camilo. "And we were on our way to rescue it."

Ontri's eyes widened and his jaw dropped. Then he furrowed his brows and pulled blunt weapons from his bag. He handed Camilo a rusted axe and Victory a broken sword. "Then let's do our best to save ourselves first."

At that moment, the wolves emerged from the trees.

Victory met the alpha's eyes, and she broke into a cold sweat. She wasn't sure if it was her impending death or just her imagination playing tricks again, but had the wolf actually smirked?

In her distraction, a young male wolf lunged for her, but Camilo pushed her out of the way. He attempted to block the wolf with the axe, but the wolf, dark furred with a contrasting light-colored streak, grabbed the handle in his mouth and pushed Camilo down.

"Camilo!" cried Victory.

Other young wolves followed his lead, despite the leader's growling and barking.

Ontri trembled as he grabbed the straps of his duffel bag. With a grunt, he swung it toward the oncoming wolves. They jumped backed and hesitated to join their pack brother as Ontri continued swinging his makeshift weapon.

Camilo struggled against the wolf, and Victory was overcome with desperation to help her friend. *I need to save him. Please, God, let me save him!*

Without thinking, she inhaled deeply and breathed a string of mint-green fire at the wolf, singeing its face.

It whimpered as it jumped off Camilo and backed away. It pawed at its snout, and the smell of burnt fur wafted through the air.

Victory blinked, bewildered. She couldn't believe what she'd done. She'd been able to not only control her fire but use it to her advantage.

Her companions, as well as the wolves, were also in awe of her dragon's breath.

Before the wolves could move again, she set the grass ablaze with her green fire, creating a wall between them and the wolves. Through the flames, she met the alpha's eyes again and flashed him a confident warning.

The leader growled but backed up to retreat. The others followed suit, but the young wolf Victory had injured hesitated.

She helped Camilo up. "Are you okay? Are you hurt?" She looked him up and down with her brows drooping. Then she noticed his coat was covered in dirt.

"Watch out!" yelled Ontri.

They turned to see the young wolf with the light streak jump over the green wall of fire, ignoring the sting of the fire singeing his stomach. The wolves cried and barked worriedly and angrily. He lunged for Victory, but Ontri swung his bag at him, pushing him off the cliff into the flowing river below.

They looked over the edge to see him float to the surface. He tried to fight against the current but to no avail; he was quickly swept away. The other wolves whined as they retreated into the trees.

"Thanks," Victory said to Ontri, who replied with a satisfied smile. She turned back to Camilo and noticed his dirty coat again. "Camilo, your coat . . ." She looked at it guiltily.

"What?" he asked, confused. He looked down, and his breath caught at the sight of the dirty splotches covering the sleeves. He quickly took it off and examined the back, which was coated in a thin layer of dirt. His jaw gaped a bit, and for a moment he was stunned silent.

"I'm so sorry," apologized Victory.

Camilo recomposed himself and shook his head. "No, no. Don't worry. I'll wash it when we get home." He gave her a warm smile. "The important thing is that you're safe."

"Thank you," she said softly, her voice breaking a little.

He rested his hand on her shoulder. "You did a good job, Victory."

For a moment, she saw Father Isaac in his proud smile. She blinked a few tears. "Thanks."

"So . . ."

She flinched and turned to Ontri, realizing she had a lot of explaining to do. "Uh . . ." She hesitated. "I can explain. You don't have to be afraid of me."

Ontri laughed. "What? I'm not afraid of you. You saved us! I think it's pretty cool that you breathe fire." He smiled widely.

Victory's eyes widened and welled up. She was so overwhelmed with relief and happiness that she didn't even try to stop the tears from falling.

Ontri freaked out. "What's wrong? Don't cry!" He turned to Camilo with a furrowed brow. "What'd I say?"

Camilo smiled knowingly and patted Victory's back to help calm her down. "She's happy you called her cool," he joked.

The real reason for her tears was that she was happy and thankful to be alive and appreciated as she was, dragon ancestry and all.

As Victory calmed down, they heard the dragon's roar echo in the chilly wind. It was the weakest they had heard yet.

"We have to hurry," said Victory with a sniff. She turned to Ontri. "I'm sorry, Ontri, but we can't go with you to Wake Zost. We have to resuce the dragon before it's too late. It's already so weak, and if we waste any more time—"

"Let's go, then."

Camilo and Victory looked at him with wide eyes. "Let's?" asked Camilo. "Don't you have to get to Wake Zost?"

"That can wait, but the dragon can't." His eyes grew determined. "I want to help."

Camilo and Victory looked at each other and decided to let Ontri join them.

"Let's go save a dragon," Victory said.

They risked cutting through the forest to save time, and Victory thanked God that they didn't encounter any dangerous creatures. *Maybe word spread that they shouldn't fight me unless they want to get burned.* She smiled proudly and held onto her stone necklace as she ran through the forest.

Within a few hours, they had trekked up the mountain. They stopped to take a break at a fork while Victory inspected the surroundings to figure out where to go next. The half-moon provided little light to guide her, and all the rocks meshed together into one giant, indiscernible heap. *Which way do we go?*

Suddenly, she detected an unfamiliar smell that she could only describe as fire and leather. "Do you guys smell that?"

Her companions sniffed the air, but they only smelled the mountain air.

"What is it?" she wondered aloud. She took a deep breath and it hit her. The dragon! It had to be! "It's this way. Come on!" She motioned for them to follow her.

At long last, they turned a corner and saw it, curled and huddled against the mountain. It was the most beautiful and stunning creature Victory had ever seen. Even in the dim light, its red scales shone, and five yellow gems glistened atop its head. Burgundy horns lined its back, while dulled metal lined the edges of its wings and wrapped around its feet and long tail. It had sustained some scratches and bruising, but the real concern was the metal end of one wing; it was bent and twisted, preventing it from flying.

The mountain was too steep for it to climb, and without any caves for it to seek refuge in, it was stuck. It growled lowly upon seeing them. Its eyes, a mix of oranges and yellows, squinted with distrust. It tried to stand, but its damaged wing wouldn't let it.

"No, wait. We're here to help." Camilo looked to Victory. "Isn't there any way you can communicate with it?"

Doubt crept through her again. How could she communicate with such a mystical and wonderful creature? She had no such gift. Only patches of scales and a fire she couldn't fully control without the help of her stone necklace.

My necklace! She held it in her hands and thought of Father Isaac. He believed in her. He wouldn't have sent her on such a crazy adventure if he hadn't known she could do it.

She swallowed down her fears and doubts and closed her eyes. She remembered the melody she had heard as a child, the one that had comforted her and lulled her to sleep on her last night alone in the wild.

"*La . . . vae . . . rae . . . oh . . .*" she sang quietly.

The dragon grunted and stared at Victory.

"*Ooh . . . neh . . . yo . . .*" Victory sang louder and dared to move closer to the majestic beast.

It grunted, but not threateningly, and relaxed as Victory sang.

She was close enough then to touch the dragon, and she rested her hand on its neck. Its skin was surprisingly smooth, unlike her own rough scales. The dragon's breath tickled her face. She turned to the boys. "It's okay."

Camilo got to work brewing a healing potion using the evenroot they had found that afternoon and asked Ontri for some of the glowing blue mushrooms to strengthen its defenses, but he couldn't take his attention off the wing. "Victory, this potion will bring back its strength, but it still won't be able to fly with its wing like that."

Victory looked at the damaged wing and bit her lip. "You're right."

"I can help with that." Ontri took a large hammer and some scrap metal from his duffel bag.

"That's why it was so heavy." Camilo rubbed his shoulder. "How can you even carry that thing?"

"Years of work." Ontri laughed. Then he sighed deeply before moving cautiously toward the dragon. He swallowed hard. "Here I go." He raised the hammer over his shoulder and brought it down with all his strength.

The dragon reeled in pain and let out a horrible shriek. All three of them covered their ears. Then the dragon growled and lunged its head toward Ontri, but Victory moved between them with her arms open wide.

"Wait! Wait! He's helping!" She sang again, and the dragon huffed but relaxed again, readying itself for the next swing.

As Ontri worked on the wing, Victory sang to comfort the dragon. It dug its claws into the ground and growled softly. Suddenly, it sniffed the air and let out a grunt, then a roar. It stared angrily beyond the cliff's edge.

Victory moved to the edge of the mountain and saw light coming from below. Worse, she saw torches. She gasped as she realized they had to be poachers.

"They're after the dragon! We have to stop them!"

"How?" Camilo asked. "You can't take them all with your slingshot alone."

"I'll use my fire."

"No. Then they'll go after you too."

"Well, we have to do something." Her eyebrows slumped with anxious worry.

"Here," said Ontri. He opened his bag and produced a round bomb almost as big as his head. "This should stop them, or at least buy us some time."

Camilo laughed. "What else are you hiding in there? What are you even doing with that?"

"I was going to trade it for some rare ingredients. But this is more important."

"But how are we going to light—"

Victory met Camilo's eyes and smiled knowingly. She took the bomb and moved to the side of the cliff that would block their path. When she was ready, she took in a deep breath and lit the bomb. Then she tossed it up the side of the mountain face and ducked. She heard the deafening explosion of rock and felt the ground shake under her feet. She turned in time to see the cliff break apart and watched as rocks tumbled to the path below, blocking the poachers' path with a mountain of stone and rubble. They wouldn't be getting to the dragon any time soon. Victory returned to the dragon's side and continued singing.

Finally, Ontri finished straightening out the wing, but he still needed to weld a new patch of metal where some had been ripped off. "Victory, mind giving me a hand? Better yet, some fire?"

Victory went to Ontri. When he told her to, she blew her green fire to melt the scrap metal onto the wing. The new metal shone against the original weathered metal around it. Then it was Camilo's turn to spread the evenroot potion on its scratches, bruises, and refurbished wing.

When they finished, the dragon flapped its wing to show that it was fixed. Wide smiles spread across all their faces. The dragon let out a roar, but unlike the pained ones from before, it was one of pure joy. Then it lay close to the ground and leaned its wing toward them.

They looked between each other with raised brows.

"You need to hurry and leave before the poachers get here," Victory warned, motioning it away with her hands.

The dragon held its position and locked eyes with her.

"Oh." She looked at the mixture of oranges and yellows that made up its eyes and understood what it wanted. She turned to her companions with a bright expression. "It's going to give us a ride."

Their eyes widened—Camilo's with excitement and Ontri's with worry.

"Really?" asked Camilo.

"You sure that's a good idea?" asked Ontri.

"You want to walk all the way back down?" Victory responded.

Ontri glanced over the edge of the high cliff. "Not really."

"Then let's go!" said Camilo.

They climbed on the dragon's back. Victory, in the front, held onto the smooth, cool red scales.

It flapped its wings to gain traction, toppling small loose rocks with its powerful gusts, and lifted itself up into the boundless sky.

They screamed with excitement and fear. Ontri clutched tightly to Camilo, to the latter's amusement.

The dragon circled a few times, roaring and howling with new energy. Then it perched on a cliff and turned its face to Victory for direction.

"You can drop us off at the bottom of the mountain there," she said, pointing.

The dragon cocked its head.

"Take us down there." She emphasized each word as she signaled in an elaborate and grand manner.

It nodded and glided gracefully through the air. The wind brushed their faces with a cool sensation and lifted Victory's three braids behind her, nearly hitting Camilo.

"Everything looks so small from up here," she said, looking below at the forest she had once feared.

"And big," added Camilo, looking toward the far-off horizon.

"You guys can tell me what it looks like after we land," Ontri said, his eyes closed.

They chuckled at his reaction.

So this is what it feels like to fly, thought Victory. It was as if the wind rushing past her took her worries with it. Her heart was comforted, and she felt at peace. She looked up to the clearing sky and whispered, "Thank you."

When the dragon landed, the ground quaked beneath its power.

The trio slid off, and Victory petted the dragon one last time before it raised its head and roared in a rhythmic tune.

"It's singing," Victory said with wonder.

After a few verses, the dragon flew away, letting out one last long roar as it disappeared against the rising sun.

"I think it said thank you," Victory said.

"You're welcome!" yelled Ontri. He waved his arms enthusiastically. His companions chuckled warmly.

"Did you guys make a wish?" asked Victory.

Camilo raised a brow. "A wish?"

"When a dragon sings, wishes and prayers come true. At least, that's the myth."

He shrugged. "Couldn't hurt."

"I wish I could continue to eat with you guys," Ontri said solemnly, looking at the rising sun. He turned to them and smiled warmly. "This was a lot of fun. Scary at times, but fun." He laughed.

Victory looked at Camilo, who nodded knowingly. She turned to Ontri. "Would you like to?"

His eyes widened.

"The church would be blessed to have a skilled cook like you," said Camilo.

Ontri's face lit up, and his eyes welled with tears. "Really?"

Victory smiled. "Yeah! Let's go home together."

As they made their way back, Camilo asked Victory, "What did you wish for?"

Victory thought of her home in Seria Longpointe and of the people she loved. She thought of her new friends, Camilo and Ontri. She thought of her green fire and scales, which she used to be ashamed of but was now thankful for. She thought of the magnificent dragon and how amazing it was to soar through the sky. She looked at Camilo and smiled playfully.

"It's a secret."

A Satyr's Lament

Kimberly Gail

I know this might be hard for you, as a human, to understand. Most of you think life for satyrs like me, and for all other Mythos, is some magically enchanted fairy tale, and that nothing could be better than that. Well, let me tell you, it's not the happily-ever-after you think it is.

Because all satyrs are male, we have to marry and mate with humans. The problem with marrying a human woman is finding one who is willing. I mean, we're not exactly high on anyone's attractiveness scale. The horns? They don't hurt. Hell, if anything, chicks seem to dig them. But a giant goat ass? That's a deal breaker.

Now, I know what you're thinking. You're a satyr, Steve; you have magic for that.

And yeah, you're right, satyrs have the ability to entrance women. We secrete a sort of musky essence that lures females faster than a spritz of Polo in a shopping mall, circa 1986. There is also what is known as satyr charm, which is this supposed ability we have to talk women into anything. That one's been blown way out of proportion. We are a bit more charming than the average male, but when you look like we do, you damn well better have a great personality.

Then there's the big one: music. That's where the true magic lies. When we sing or play instruments, we become unavoidably irresistible.

And I mean that literally. They cannot resist. Women are entranced by the music and will do anything asked of them.

I once asked my dad, "Doesn't the whole entrancing thing feel kind of skeezy to you? Isn't it basically the Mythos version of slipping something in a girl's drink?"

His response was, "Go ask your mother."

But when I continued to stand there glaring at him, he set down his pen and gave me a real answer.

"Look at me."

Dad's not attractive, even by satyr standards. His ashy-brown hair is thin and oily, his nostrils are too wide, and the skin around his eyes is always puffy. This isn't just because he's middle-aged, either. I've seen the pictures; he's always looked that way.

"Do you think a beautiful woman like your mother would have given me the time of day? Hell, no! So yeah, I cranked up the satyr essence and played a little uke for her."

He paused at the mention of his uke and got a little misty-eyed. Dad was a ukulele fanatic. There had been times I thought he loved his uke more than he loved me or my brother, Sami. For most of my childhood, he had carried that damn thing strapped to his back everywhere he went. When I was twelve, he tried to teach me to play. I was incapable of creating anything but cringe-inducing noise with it. In my frustration, I smashed the shit out of that thing.

I shrugged and gave Dad my best *I'm still sorry about that* face, and he continued his story.

"I used all the satyr charms to get her to notice me. Once she was willing to pay attention to me, I backed off the magic and just let her get to know me. In the end, she decided she liked me enough that the horns and goat's ass didn't matter."

"Seriously?" I asked, looking at the rest of him.

"What can I say?" he quipped. "I am just that cool a guy." With that, he picked up his pen and went back to work writing jingles.

So anyway, yes, it's true; satyrs have magic to attract women. So why don't I just rely on that magic? Because I don't have it. I can't sing, and musical instruments are totally beyond me. I already mentioned my dad's ukulele, right? Yeah, it's been that way with any instrument I've tried. I am completely and utterly tone-deaf. I couldn't tell you the difference between a-flat, c-sharp, and x-squared.

And it doesn't stop there. That legendary satyr charm? That's a no-go for me. Sure, I can be witty and charming with people I know. But strangers? Nah, man, I've got way too much anxiety for that. And it doesn't do much good to lure a girl in with your musk if you're just going to get all tongue-tied when you try to talk to her.

I'm a tone-deaf half-man/half-goat with major social anxiety. So basically, when it comes to love, I'm fucked.

Case in point, a few years ago, when I was still a teenager, I came up with the idea of using the music I had downloaded on my phone to entrance this girl I liked. At that point, I had figured it was mostly the musk we emit that really woos the girls and that music was, well, just music. So I played her this really great song by this amazing band I liked called Bananas Fawster and turned on the satyr musk.

We danced real close. I mean, *real* close. The kind of dancing that, to a teenage boy, is basically foreplay but, you know, with a couple of layers of clothes between you. But when I tried to kiss her, she shut me down quick.

For the next few days, she wasn't at school. By the next week, word had gotten out that she had run away to follow Bananas Fawster around on tour. So my idea worked out great for those guys. All it did for me was teach me the importance of a satyr's music.

My dad has a theory as to why my satyr magic is lacking. He thinks it's because I'm a second son, which is rare. Most of our kind only ever have one child. My mom told me that's because once you've had a fat furry ass and a set of hooves come kicking out of your vagina, you're not exactly keen on the idea of ever having to experience it again. I can see her point. But it obviously didn't stop her from having a second child.

I apparently owe my existence to my brother, Sami. Mom said she had never seen a more adorable child and that his voice was the most beautiful thing she'd ever heard. I guess she wanted a pair of perfect children instead of just one, so she chose to push out another set of hooves and horns. And for all her effort, she got me. So that backfired on her.

Yeah, yeah . . . I'm not a bad-looking guy. Well, not from the waist up, anyway. But I know the fact that I can't carry a tune disappointed Mom for a long time. She kind of got over it when Sami made it big, though. At one point, she told me she was glad she had one "normal" child because she couldn't handle having two rock stars in the family. I would have been insulted, but I think she genuinely meant it as a compliment.

I don't need to ask if you know who my brother is, do I? Ha! No, of course not; everyone knows Sami.

But no one knows him like I do. There's just something about brothers, you know? And like I said before, a second son is rare. So for a satyr, having a brother is like its own kind of magic. For a kid like me, without the regular magic, that's meant a lot.

Growing up, Sami never let any of the others satyrs give me shit, either. If they tried, he'd knock the crap out of them. And then he taught me to knock the crap out of them myself.

When we got a little older, there was this guy, Alkaios, who was an absolute ass to me over the whole lacking magic thing. He was way too big to beat up. I tried; it didn't go well. If you look close enough, you'll see my nose is a little crooked. That was Alkaios.

Sami was determined to not only get the guy off my back but also get back at him for breaking my nose. So he set out to steal his girlfriend. It really didn't take much effort for him. Our mom wasn't the only female to think his was the most beautiful voice in the world. And if Alkaios got a new girlfriend, Sami would steal her away too. Ha, ha! No one else had magic as strong as his. Alkaios finally swore to leave me alone forever if Sami would quit interfering with his love life.

I would have done anything to thank my brother for getting that jerk off my case, but he just smiled and said, "Anything for you, k-i-i-i-i-i-d," in this ridiculous impersonation of a goat he liked to do. It was the dumbest thing ever, but it always made me laugh.

People have always asked if I'm jealous of Sami's success, and the answer is a strong no. I've always been proud of him. I looked up to him—not because he was a great singer, just because he was great. He was the one person who always challenged me to see the greatness in myself. And when I couldn't, he'd find it for me.

He was the first person I ever let read my poetry. Well, technically, he found my notebook and read it without my permission. But instead of making fun of me for it, he encouraged me to write more. "This is where your magic hides," he said.

Of course, I misunderstood him at first. I tried reading my poems at some of those underground poetry reading things, thinking I'd finally found the secret of my satyr magic. There was this really hot girl in the crowd, and I upped my musk, used my most charming voice, and looked her right in the eye as I read my favorite poem. I thought for sure she'd be all over me when I stepped off the stage. But when I walked up to her afterward and laid my best pickup line on her, she laughed so hard that she spewed her drink in my face.

My poetry was not real magic. Not for me, anyway.

But for Sami, my words did work magic. He asked me if he could use one of my poems to write a song. I was so damn flattered he liked it that much that of course I agreed. His first big hit, "If You Would Be Loved"? I wrote those lyrics.

Sami tried getting me a few dates after that by telling some of his fans that I wrote the words to his new hit. I actually thought that might be the secret to breaking the curse of my love life.

It wasn't. Sometimes a girl would act like she was interested in me, but she really just wanted to get close to my brother. They might have been my words, but Sami was the one who sang them and that's where the magic was.

After that, I decided to just forget about poetry and women. I thought about becoming a monk. I told my dad my new plan over breakfast the next day. And that's when he told me that not only are monks sworn off women, but they're not even allowed to touch themselves. Considering it was 10 a.m. and I'd already broken that rule twice, I decided that wasn't the life for me.

It turns out that whole monk idea wouldn't have played out anyway because that was the day I met Angie. I was walking across campus when I heard some sort of rally going on. My natural instinct is to ignore those things. A good 70 percent of rallies are aimed at placing some sort of restrictions on Mythos or at trying to ban us outright. Who needs that shit right after breakfast?

But I saw a few Mythos moving toward the rally with interested expressions rather than the bitter anger that appears right before you start arguing with fanatics about your right to exist. It piqued my own interest enough to make me look that way. That's when I saw Angie, brown curls whipping in the wind, megaphone in hand, fervidly calling out for compassion and acceptance for a group of furies who had recently been arrested on campus. Considering the furies are vengeful assassins, that's kind of a hard sell. But there she was, all five foot two of her, fighting for the rights of these Mythos who had, in her words, "only been protecting an abused girl."

I completely missed the class I'd been rushing toward. I pushed my way toward the front of the crowd instead and spent the hour staring into the intense green eyes of this fiery little champion of my people. It turned out she was championing more for women than for Mythos, but it didn't matter. I was ready to follow any cause she was a part of.

After that, if I walked past a rally, I made sure I looked to see who was talking and what it was about. Most of them were still anti-Mythos. But from time to time, I would see Angie, and if she was there, the topic was always something to do with women's or equal rights. At the end of one of them, I overheard her and some others talking about planning a protest outside a major corporation known for paying women half of what they pay men.

When I heard them say something about needing volunteers, I shouted out, "I'll help!" I don't know who was more shocked by that sudden outburst: the girls I'd been eavesdropping on or my own socially anxious self.

After their initial wariness of me, they realized I was sincere enough and let me volunteer. I think they were still suspicious of my motives until I showed up at the protest with my mom in tow. An adoring mother is going to do one of two things. Either she's going to kill your chances with a girl by making it seem like you're some sort of sad-sack mama's boy who will never leave home, or she'll convince a girl that you're sweet for spending time with your poor, lonely mom.

My mom fucking rocks! I know because I'm a total mama's boy, but she made all the girls think I'm some totally independent superstar who still makes time for his mother. Basically, she's the best wingman ever.

So the girls liked me then, including Angie. And I liked all of them. I call them the rally girls. They were a good group of friends. Of course, by that point, I was half in love with Angie, but the anxiety kept me from asking her out. I'd just get too damn nervous around her when I started thinking about it. Then I'd get anxiety sweat.

Have you ever smelled anxiety sweat? Well, in your line of work, I'm sure you have. Smells like a goat's ass, right? Yeah, now imagine getting that when you actually have a goat's ass. There was no way I was going to be getting any dates with all that going on. But we were friends and that was good enough. I just wanted to spend time with her.

She confided in me once that when I'd first volunteered, she thought I was trying to work some angle. The fact that I was a satyr had had her defenses up. Obviously, I'm not the only one to ever question the sleaziness of the satyr magic. It seemed perfectly logical to me that this girl who fights so hard for women's rights would have those same questions. It didn't even bother me that she'd thought I was up to something.

But then she started crying and apologizing for falling victim to the sheep mentality and letting herself be influenced by stereotypes. She was so outraged at herself that she started to get me a little pissed off at her for it too. But when she looked at me with her sad eyes and pouty lip, I forgot all about being mad. All I wanted to do was kiss her, and I knew she felt so guilty, she'd probably let me. Then I was pissed at myself for thinking that way. It was just the type of thing she was apologizing to me for having assumed.

She had my brain in knots. I was an absolute fucking mess. And that's when I knew for sure that I was in love with her.

A couple of weeks after that, we watched the news together so we could hear the verdict from the trial of the furies she'd been rallying for. I'd been hoping for a not-guilty verdict so I could ask Angie out on a date while she was all caught up in the excitement. Instead, I ended up holding her for hours while she wept in my arms. We'd known they were likely to be found guilty. But the death sentence? That was a punch to the gut we hadn't expected.

I didn't see her again for a while after that. Not because I didn't want to, but because she'd locked herself away from the world. She said she couldn't face such a horrible place until she took some time to heal. I was concerned about her, but I knew the rally girls were taking care of her, so I knew I didn't really have to worry. They'd get her through it. But it was kind of a shot to the heart that she kept me on the outside with the rest of the world.

A couple of months later, I ran into the rally girls on campus. They told me Angie was slowly making her way back into the world. She was actually going to some poetry reading thing at a dive bar a few blocks off campus that night. They asked if I wanted to meet them there. After my previous experience, a poetry reading sounded like something I would enjoy about as much as a twelve-mile hike through the seventh level of Hell.

I told them I would see them there.

No way was I going to miss a chance to see Angie.

I wasn't sure how she would react to seeing me there. I mean, it wasn't she who had invited me. There was a chance she'd be pissed that the rally girls had asked me to come.

But when she saw me, she ran up to me and crushed me in a hug. Then she kissed me on the cheek and thanked me for respecting her enough to give her time to heal. I never really saw that I had a choice in the matter, but if it landed me a hug and a kiss, I wasn't going to argue.

The poetry reading ended up being not as hellish as I had anticipated. Probably because I got to just sit and listen and wasn't forced to take part. Sure, a lot of the poetry sucked, but some of it was pretty amazing. Angie read something she'd written during her self-imposed isolation. It wasn't the best work of the night, but it was far from the worst and it was an expression of her heart, so that made it worthwhile to me.

The rally girls asked me if I ever wrote poetry, and I told them that I used to. I even let it slip that the lyrics to "If You Would Be Loved" were from a poem I'd written. Of course, they didn't believe me. And that's when I told them about Sami being my brother, which they didn't believe either. Even when I showed them his contact info and a picture of us together in my phone, they refused to believe it. A call to my mom . . . that's what convinced them.

I don't usually tell people about Sami being my brother because it leads to them trying to use me to get closer to him. But Angie and the rally girls were different. That kind of thing didn't matter to them. And they were way more impressed that I'd written "If You Would Be Loved" than they were by Sami. It was an amazing night. I started writing poetry again after that.

The timing of me outing myself as the brother of a rock star couldn't have been more fortuitous. Sami called just a few days later to say he was coming to town. He'd been on tour for over a year, the past few months of which were overseas. He hadn't been due to come back for another month, but there was some issue with his drummer's passport and they had to cancel their last few concerts.

It just so happened that I was at a meeting for some benefit thing Angie and the rally girls were planning when Sami called. They'd been discussing the need for entertainment to draw people in. I don't know what the hell I was thinking, but I suddenly heard myself asking my brother if he'd be willing to sing a few songs at a women's rights benefit. The shocked looks on the faces of the rally girls told me just how nuts my request was. I had just asked the biggest name in rock to play in a college auditorium to a couple hundred activists at an anti-sexism rally. There was no way in hell he would actually want to do that.

Through the phone, I heard laughter followed by "Anything for you, k-i-i-i-i-i-d."

Angie smiled and gave me a bone-crushing hug. Before I left, she told me she was looking forward to meeting Sami because if he was anything like me, he had to be amazing. Unlike anyone else from my life, ever, I was actually excited to introduce Angie to my brother. It wasn't until I got home that I realized she had basically called me amazing. My love life didn't feel quite so hopeless anymore.

It was getting so much easier to talk to Angie, but for some reason, I still couldn't get past the hurdle of asking her out. My mom suggested I invite her over for dinner. After a minute or two of me staring at her in horror, she told me that if Sami was going to do the benefit, he would have to meet Angie and discuss logistics anyway. So why not do it over dinner? There was something about it not being a date that made it possible for me to call and invite her. The smug look my mom had on her face for the rest of the day told me she had known that all along.

Sometimes, my wingman is a bit sneaky.

The dinner went great. Angie showed up looking more beautiful than ever, and she gave me a hug and a kiss on the cheek again when she came in. Things were definitely looking up for me. My family even did their best not to embarrass me. Dad didn't try to show off by singing any of his commercial jingles, which he normally did whenever we had company. And my mom tried to subtly talk up my accomplishments in school while downplaying Sami's musical success. It earned her a couple of side-eyes from him, but he understood why she did it. At least, I thought he did.

Sami asked Angie what the benefit was all about, and she explained they were trying to start a fund to pay legal fees for people like the furies. She went into great detail about how unfair it was for them to be sentenced to death for defending and protecting abused women and that competent legal representation could have prevented that sentence.

At that point, Sami commented that he wasn't sure how castrating a man who then bled to death translated into defending and protecting. But Angie had been fighting this fight for a long time now, and she was ready with an argument of her own. Something to the effect of the death being unintentional and a repeat offender never being able to repeat his offense again.

Sometimes, I think she may have a little fury blood of her own. Anyway, she had him agreeing it was a good cause and that he was happy to help out and play a few songs if it would help. They actually came up with a pretty good plan for him to play a couple of songs in between each of the speakers who were planning to present that night. They figured people would be willing to stick around longer if they spread the entertainment out over the course of the night.

My mom asked her who was speaking and on what topics. Angie told her about a few of the topics, including her own speech on the misconceptions of abstinence. She explained that there was a prevalent view in society that remaining chaste and women's rights didn't go together. That the double standards by which men have the freedom to do whatever they want while women are often shamed for promiscuity led many to believe that chastity was a form of subjugation to a male-minded society.

"But it is and always should be a woman's right to choose," Angie insisted. "One choice is no more valid than the other. But just as a woman should never be shamed for choosing to have sex, she should also never be shamed for choosing not to." She went on to talk about her own vow of chastity.

By the end of that dinner, I loved Angie more than ever.

But while the dinner went great, things got a little weird afterward. I asked Sami what he thought of Angie, and he laughed. When I asked what was so funny, he said, "You finally get a girl to like you and she's a total prude."

"She's not a prude," I argued. "She's choosing to remain a virgin until she's married. I think it's admirable."

He laughed harder.

"Laugh all you want," I told him, "but I think she's strong and courageous. She's amazing. And while I hope to marry the girl someday, I'm fine with her vow even if that never happens."

Sami shook his head and walked away, muttering something about sampling the goods as he went. It was the first time I had ever wanted to lock horns with my own brother.

Things with Sami seemed to get better before the benefit. In fact, I read him the poem that Angie wanted me to read at the event, which is something only she could have convinced me to do. He said it was my best work since "If You Would Be Loved." He asked if I wanted him to play guitar in the background while I read it. Having him there with me would make it easier for me to go through with the reading, so of course I said, "Hell, yeah."

And it did help. I wasn't anxious at all while I did my reading. I'm sure it was because most eyes were on Sami. That satyr music will almost always steal the show. But when I was done, I had several people telling me how great my poem was. Hell, Sami even said he thought he could turn it into his next big hit. I was flying pretty high at that point.

I went out for some air, and when I came back in, a couple of the rally girls were giving a presentation on the furies and their lack of competent representation. I listened to their speech in its entirety and then looked around for Angie. I didn't see her anywhere. Then I remembered her speech would be coming up soon, so I knew she would probably be in the back, preparing. I decided to go find Sami and see if he wanted to listen to her talk with me.

When I walked into Sami's dressing room and saw Angie on her knees, naked . . . I froze. I just couldn't process what I was seeing. What she was doing to him . . . it just wasn't something she would do. It went against everything she believed in. I thought about every cause I'd seen her rally for and every speech I'd heard her make. Hell, she was due to give a speech on abstinence in fifteen minutes. And that's when I knew. It wasn't her! Not really. He'd entranced her. My own fucking brother had used satyr magic to exploit and control the girl he *knew* I loved!

When Sami saw me, he laughed. And then the bastard had the audacity to say, "I guess some vows are made to be broken. You want me to have her do you next, little brother? She'll totally do it if I tell her to."

And that's when I snapped.

So to answer your question, yes, officer, I do understand my rights. But I won't remain silent because I need you and everyone else to understand just how I got here.

I loved Sami. But what he did . . .

He deserved what I did to him.

But so did the guy those furies killed. And we all know how that story ended.

A Harvest of Irony

Douglas Anstruther

"This is where they killed my mother," I said, pointing to a low rise of ground between the trees. I looked back at my young apprentice, Amelia, clutching her basket with knotted fists. I saw fear in her face.

"Ma'am, I didn't know."

"Oh? Hadn't you heard?" I circled the unmarked spot amid the falling autumn leaves. Each year, the trees tried to bury the memory of what had happened here. The rest of the village might have forgotten, but I never would.

"No, Madam Sayda. I mean, yes. It's just, I didn't know we were coming here. I thought . . ." She looked down into the empty basket.

"Yes, dear," I said. "We'll get to that. This is just a brief stop to pay our respects." I brushed the leaves off a nearby log and motioned Amelia to sit beside me. We sat there for some time before I broke the silence. "It happened twenty years ago, but I remember it perfectly."

I stared ahead, seeing once more the flames superimposed on the woods. The shadowy form of my mother writhed within them. Her screams echoed off the newly grown trees. The memory threatened to drag me back to the raw terror of that night, but I refused. I knew the flames had left only a tarry hatred that clung to everything it touched. Instead, I sampled the emotions, letting the fear and hatred linger like a taste in the mouth, using them to steel my resolve. I could not indulge them, not now, lest they unravel my magic, and I shook myself free from the memory's spell.

"The village woke us just before dawn," I continued. "They dragged my mother here, tied her to a post, and burned her to death. I was twelve, just a couple of years older than you, but it took three men to hold me back. I screamed and cried and cursed them all until I collapsed." I wondered how an older version of myself would have reacted. Knowing the futility of protests, perhaps I would have watched in silence. And planned.

"Why?" Amelia asked, her voice almost a whisper. I sensed her hesitancy, her fear of upsetting me, but curiosity had won out. "Why did they do it?" I looked down at the child and wondered how much she knew. Her mother had helped gather the firewood.

"My mother was a holy woman," I said, "like me. They burned her when the harvest failed."

"Why?" I frowned at the girl. "I mean, why did they blame her? Was it—"

"Her fault?" I finished. I looked back up at the remembered flames. "Maybe."

We spent the next two hours gathering food and ingredients for potions and salves. The early autumn forest obliged us, filling Amelia's basket. Her elaborately decorated clothes became stained from crawling through narrow spaces. My own clothes were plain and worn. Long ago, this would have been a cause for embarrassment, something I would have tried to hide, but I wore them proudly now, a mark for all to see of the hardship I had endured since my husband left me for more fertile fields. My long black hair, which Amelia had painstakingly combed and braided earlier, remained untouched by the day's exertions, while Amelia's jutted out in a mess of tangles and entwined twigs—evidence enough of our stations in life.

As we went, I taught. I explained the effects one could expect from the plants, rocks, and insects we gathered. Amelia carried the basket, and I was responsible for the waterskin and harvesting knife, which hung from my rope waistband. Amelia, the chief's niece, would serve as my apprentice for the next year, and although I didn't enjoy catering to the whims of that bloated fool, I did love my art and gladly shared it. As for the girl, she proved a capable enough student.

Amelia's biggest flaw came from her close resemblance to her cousin, Tarak: the chief's son and my former husband. Every time I looked at her, I saw his eyes. I couldn't help but think that our own child would have looked a lot like her if the gods, in their cruel irony, hadn't intervened. She was even the right age. It upset me, and I found myself avoiding her face.

In a dim patch of woods where tall trees blocked out the sun, we came across a patch of green mushrooms. They grew together in a mass, small heads on long curved stems.

"I'd hoped to find these," I said. "They're rare but useful."

"What do they do?" the girl asked as she gathered the sticky flesh into her basket.

"They treat pain."

"Oh." She sounded impressed.

"You have to be careful, though. Most people who eat them get bad stomach cramps, but they can be dangerous for someone who's old or weak."

"I thought you said you used them to treat pain."

"Yes."

"But they cause pain."

"Exactly. That's how the gods work. Trickery and cruelty are the two things you can depend on. Always remember that, Amelia, because if you understand the gods, you can predict them. And if you can predict them, you can control them."

We continued onward through the forest, stepping over fallen branches and moving around areas tangled with vines.

"The gods all want different things," I explained. "The wind wants to move and will break things that refuse it passage. Water and rocks want to fall, and fire wants to consume. My mother realized that they had no interest in our sacrifices. What good is a burnt lamb to the god of the harvest?"

Amelia began to wilt from exertion, so I sat on the leaf-strewn forest floor, detached the waterskin from my hip, and held it up to her. She sat nearby and took a long drink.

"That's why they burned her," I said. Amelia looked at me, not understanding. "My mother. She'd convinced the people to stop sacrificing to the gods and taught them to give the gods what they want instead. Fertility wants water and soil, so she had them irrigate their land and spread it with manure. For half a dozen years, the harvests increased and the people grew fat and happy.

"But then came a drought so bad that even the river dried up. All the crops died, and they went into winter with nothing. So they sacrificed her to the gods."

"Did it work?" the girl asked. I looked at her, surprised. She was quite brave, or foolish, to ask such a question.

"No. The drought worsened and continued for three more years. Their sacrifice went unanswered and nearly a quarter of the village died. When people passed me in the streets, they looked down. They knew that what they'd done to my mother, to me, had only made things worse. They'd been given a test and failed, and as punishment, they starved."

But not all the guilty were punished. Hatred and anger threatened to rise up within me again. So easy, it was, to summon those emotions; so hard to cultivate love. It was a mistake to come here, to rekindle these feelings. It risked too much. I needed discipline now more than ever.

After a pause, Amelia said softly, "My mother says your mother was a good person."

"Yes. She was," I said, feeling the pain of her loss like a weight in my chest, not lightened after all these years. "My mother always saw the good in people and in the gods. But for all her wisdom, she only saw half the truth. She didn't understand their cruelty. The day before they killed her, she promised me a special lesson. As I cried over her black, charred body, I received that lesson."

I stood and offered the girl my hand. "Come. Your basket is full. It's time to go back."

Halfway home, we heard a rustling of leaves ahead of us. It stopped, then started again: a frantic, desperate sound. We passed a patch of thick brambles and on the other side found a young deer with its back leg trapped in a V between two branches of a tree. It must have leaped over the briar and caught its leg as it came down. The deer's front legs tore at the ground, but it was unable to lift its back leg enough to free it.

I motioned for Amelia to stand back and moved slowly toward the panicked deer. It shrank back, making abrupt skittering movements to startle me away, but I kept moving forward, hands out. I put one hand on its flank, only a little higher than my waist, and continued down toward the trapped leg. It calmed as it grew accustomed to my presence. With both hands, I grasped its leg and pushed it back and up, releasing it from the tree's trap.

The creature shot forward to the edge of the clearing, where it stopped and turned to face me. I bent down and extended my left hand toward it.

I heard Amelia make a little gasp of joy as the deer walked toward me with its neck curved down. "I think it wants to thank you," she whispered.

As it came within reach, I turned my hand over to pet the short bristly hair between its eyes.

Amelia approached with her arm outstretched to pet the docile creature.

"Yes, that's right," I murmured to the beast. "You can help me with Amelia's lesson."

With my right hand, I pulled the curved knife from my waistband and, in one forceful motion, raked it across the animal's throat. A torrent of blood burst across me, and the deer collapsed to the ground like a dead man cut from a tree.

"No!" Amelia screamed and ran at me. She collided against my side, and her small hands reached for the knife. I let her take the blade, and having disarmed me, she no longer knew what to do.

The creature writhed at our feet for a moment, spraying blood in a weakening stream. Its fluid movements ceased, and a moment later, jerking spasms spread across its glassy-eyed form.

Amelia threw herself onto its warm fur and sobbed, ruining her clothes and skin with dark, sticky blood. "Why?" she demanded, straining her neck to look up at me. Disappointment and anger had drained her face of its youthful innocence.

Good.

"I wanted to show you. This is how the gods work. To be destroyed by the same hand that saves you. There's no better example."

The next evening, the village held its fall harvest celebration. Everyone gathered in the clearing at the edge of the village to share stories, sing songs, and join in the harvest feast.

I took my turn at storytelling, relating the tale of the boy who came down with spots after teasing a peculiarly spotted bird and the story of the girl who waited ten years to catch a star but found herself distracted by a handsome boy when a star finally drifted within reach. The children sat at the front, soaking in the entertainment. I saw Amelia among them, refusing to return my gaze.

After the sun set, the children disappeared, and a line of musicians assembled at the edge of the crowd. They worked their instruments in frenzied trances, weaving a powerful spell that linked the dancers to them and to each other. A bonfire lit the happy faces and twisting bodies with a red glow that moved among them like a spirit.

On a platform opposite the line of musicians, the globular form of the chief sat looking over the crowd. The man possessed the sole virtue of consistency, wearing a vapid expression at all times and reliably making the most foolish of decisions. His unceasing adoration of Tarak, his only son and heir, proved no exception. The chief had overseen a similar fire with the same vacuous look two decades before. I wondered if he even remembered killing my mother.

I stood back, away from the crowd, and scanned the flickering red faces. My heart skipped a beat before I realized that I had found Tarak grinning back at me. I'd always loved his smile, and I focused on that, forcing myself to remember all the times it had captivated me in the past.

I'd known Tarak my entire life, but when puberty transformed him from a thin, gangly boy to a muscular, broad-shouldered man with achingly beautiful eyes and wide, full lips, I fell in love. Years had passed before he felt the same. I stayed close, and we became best friends, talking for hours at a time about everything under the sun and moon. Over time, a spark of passion appeared, which I nurtured carefully into flame, like an ember on dry grass.

His father had disapproved at first, but the memory of the drought weighed on him. Eventually, he decided to welcome me into the family in the hope that it would please the gods. It could have been his one good decision if he hadn't undone it later by giving Tarak permission to leave me.

Tarak and I had married shortly after my nineteenth birthday. We had spent six years together before he renounced me and took another wife. He needed an heir, he'd said, and he couldn't wait any longer for me. The night he left had been the worst of my life. The pain of loss had competed with burning humiliation to destroy me.

For years, I hated him and his new wife. She bore Tarak five children. Each died shortly after birth, and the last child took her with him after last year's harvest.

There had been rumblings, of course, that I had been involved, that I would know just the right concoction to do the job. Unable to feign sadness, I kept to myself, spending most of my time at home or in the woods outside the village.

I hadn't seen much of Tarak while his new wife lived. At the spring celebration, we'd found each other and spent the night talking at the edge of the bonfire's light until it went out. Since then, we'd spent more and more time together as our old friendship reawakened.

Tarak worked his way through the crowd toward me, embracing some, touching a shoulder here, and taking a hand there as he went. He moved with a lithe grace completely unknown to his father. I drank it in, remembering the feeling of satisfaction I used to get from watching him perform his magic, so alien to me—a satisfaction born not from vanity or pride but from the knowledge that, yes, this man was good enough for me, for our future children.

All around, gleaming eyes watched Tarak approach. Everyone in the village admired the brave, handsome, and capable heir to the chief. Their feelings for me were more complex: equal parts fear and respect mixed in a base of guilty loathing. Yet they all came to me when they needed advice or help.

"How typical to find you here, Sayda, watching over your people from a distance," he said, standing beside me.

"*Your* people are watching over *me*. I don't think they approve of us consorting."

He gazed out across the throng. Most eyes had turned back to their own business, and the few that lingered broke off at his glance. I imagined disapproval in those watching eyes. Everyone knew that Tarak still needed an heir and believed that I was barren, Tarak among them. Only I knew the truth.

"The people respect and admire you," he said. "They hope that you will take me back."

"Oh?" I said, raising my eyebrows at his bold suggestion.

Tarak gave a charming little bow and offered both his hands. "Come," he said. "It's too crowded here."

We went to my home and made love for the first time in seven years. Although the night air stayed humid and warm, we passed the hours in a tight embrace. When passion reached its crescendo again, our sticky sweat heightened the sense of abandon.

I woke first, just before sunrise, and carefully left the bed to start a fire. The smell of cooking eggs and venison roused Tarak, and he joined me groggily for breakfast. We shared an ardent embrace and kiss before sitting down together at the small table. He ate like a starving man, while I picked at my food. Even seeing him eat brought up mixed memories. I focused on the good. After he cleared his plate, an awkward silence fell that Tarak finally broke.

"Sayda, I want you to know that I've changed. When we were together . . ." He looked down, ashamed. "Well, I wasn't dependable back then. I drank too much. When I think about our last night together, I just . . ." He shook his head.

"No. No, please. I don't want to talk about that." *I need to love you.*

"I just want you to know, I would never do anything like that again. I would never hurt you. Please believe me."

As he spoke, I stood, cleared the table, and went to the door. Outside, the cool breeze felt good on my skin. "Let's sit out here, Tarak. It's too stuffy inside."

From the top of the small hill, we could see the sun working its way up through the forest trees. On the other side, the village—a messy cluster of small homes—huddled in the smoke of morning fires. I sat on the ground with my back against a large flat rock, and Tarak laid beside me, resting his head in my lap. The morning passed quickly as the two of us laughed over shared stories and I played absently with his curls. We made plans: things we would do together, who we would tell first, where we would live. The birds chirped in the crisp fall breeze, everything felt right, and for the first time in a long time, I was happy.

Tarak moaned softly.

"What's wrong, my love?"

"Nothing," he said. "Just some stomach pain. It'll pass."

A few minutes later, he moaned again, louder, and sat up clutching his stomach. He rocked for a few minutes before the pain passed and he returned his head to my lap, this time facing me.

We talked more about what the village would think of us. He looked thoughtful, and a frown of worry darkened his face. "My father won't approve, of course. He insists I must have an heir." He looked up into my eyes. "But some things are more important. I love you, Sayda. That's all that matters."

"I'm not barren," I said quietly. Tears started working their way down my cheek.

"But—"

"We still have time," I said. "Time for children, lots of them."

Tarak sat up in surprise. "But you never . . . when?"

"That night. That terrible night. I was going to tell you that I was pregnant, but you weren't in the mood to listen."

A spasm of pain curled him into a ball beside my legs. I got onto my knees, leaned forward, and rubbed his head and back until it passed. When it did, he turned to me and said hoarsely, "What happened?"

I straightened my back, wiped the tears from my face, and looked him in the eyes. "You beat me so badly I lost the baby."

Realization washed over him. "No," he whispered.

"Shhh," I said, cupping his head between my arm and chest. "Shhh. We mustn't think about any of that now. We need to focus on the future, not the past. I love you, Tarak."

And I truly did.

Because an hour later he lay dead in my arms.

The gods, in their cruel predictability, had taken him from me. The sticky green mushrooms only killed the sick and frail, but I knew that if I loved him—*really* loved him—the gods wouldn't be able to resist the temptation. I had lured them with dangled bait, and they had acted. His death rested on their hands.

I held his lifeless body and sobbed uncontrollably. Our joyful reunion announcement would never happen. Never again would we stay up late talking or making love. We would never have children. Slowly, the fantasies faded and I turned to the practical lessons of the past. The memories I had so carefully avoided these last months returned in full force: his drunken rages, the beatings, and the infidelities. In truth, he had been dead to me since the night he took our child's life. But one could love the dead, just as one could simultaneously hate and love the living.

My tears ceased, and I looked at him with a calm satisfaction. The village would pay in heartache, and the chief would learn what it felt like to lose the one person who mattered most. By cultivating my love for Tarak, I had moved the gods to dispense justice where they'd offered only spite before.

If you understood the gods, you could predict them. And if you could predict them, you could control them.

Jane Quits Inhuman Resources

Lydia Bugg

It was the worst floor in the entire building, possibly one of the worst places in the entire world. Although we're not yet aware of life on other planets, if there were, it's entirely likely that they might come to Earth in order to declare floor seven of the Mystichem building the worst place in the entire universe.

It was always damp. The running theory was that it had something to do with both the air-conditioning and heating systems being simultaneously broken. This also had the side effect that there was no season in which it was ever a comfortable temperature. In winter, it was freezing, and the moist floors were slick. In the summer, the muggy air created a tropical climate, which also tended to attract creatures, mostly howler monkeys, which nested in the ceilings.

The howler monkeys created a whole different problem because no matter how many times Jane appealed to the company to have them removed, the response was always that they could not be because they were endangered. Apparently, they had resided in the ceiling of the seventh floor of Mystichem for so long that it was now scientifically classified as their natural environment. As such, removal of the howler monkeys would be a federal offense.

Most people thought howler monkeys made a shrieking noise, but the low, throaty sounds they emitted were more similar to a Gregorian chant, or a frat boy burping for an extended period of time. Either way, it was a particularly unpleasant sound.

It wasn't just the dampness or the monkeys or the lights that turned on and off as they pleased. Jane didn't like the seventh floor mainly because of the isolation. She was the only employee of the Chicago office's Inhuman Resources department. There were several branch offices in abandoned warehouses, under bridges, and in haunted libraries all across town. There was even one employee who worked from home, though they only let him do that because his home was a tomb he had been imprisoned in since 1745. He often tried to trick his coworkers into freeing him for meetings.

Jane was a social woman, and it was very annoying to her that the only place she ever saw her coworkers was in her dreams, which was where they had meetings. Specifically, in *her* dreams. They were supposed to rotate whose dreams they had their weekly staff meeting in, but they seemed to come to her much more frequently than anyone else. One moment Ryan Gosling would be spoon-feeding her Neapolitan ice cream and brushing her hair, the next she would be surrounded by her coworkers. It was horribly embarrassing.

The coalition of all these points made her decide to quit her job, which she had done twelve previous times. Her manager, Monty, always seemed to find a way to talk her into staying. He would give her a raise or a title bump or a new parking space or a tiny mariachi outfit to put on her favorite howler monkey, and she would found herself right back at work. Today would be different, though. Today would be the day she finally quit her job!

It was time for her quarterly review, so she drank a large glass of milk and read the manual for her microwave oven before bed in hopes that she would have very boring dreams. She found herself jumping on a trampoline with a sloth similar to the one on her pink sloth pajamas, which she was still wearing in the dream. Just as the sloth was about to hand her a bowl of Neapolitan ice cream, Monty appeared. He was in his customary business suit, and he jumped very seriously, his briefcase clutched to his side.

"Good evening, Jane. Jane's friend," he said, addressing the sloth.

"That's a sloth, Monty," Jane said.

"I don't care who you make friends with, Jane," Monty replied. "I myself have many friends who only defecate once a week."

"He's part of my dream; we're not here together."

"Oh, good. Because while I don't care who you make friends with, it would be extremely inappropriate to bring a friend to your quarterly performance review, which this now is." He snapped his fingers, and they were in his office, a darkened void populated only by the large desk Monty sat behind and a single black office chair.

Jane felt underdressed in her sloth pajamas. "Good. I've been looking forward to this meeting. I emailed you a PowerPoint presentation at around ten. Could you please pull it up?"

"Certainly." He placed the bowl of ice cream on the table and slid it across to her. "I saved this for you."

Jane picked up the spoon and dug out a generous bite.

Monty pulled up the PowerPoint entitled "I'm quitting again by Jane Forest-Links." He quickly closed it.

"I'm sorry, Jane, but I just can't let you quit. You are my best worker. You're always on time, you're great at your job, and you've never dissolved into a puddle of green slime. Have I told you about the issues we're having with Nancy? Don't even get me started."

"I understand your position, but you have to understand that I'm not happy. I'm horribly lonely and extremely damp, and Robert ate most of his mariachi outfit. I'm unhappy, and I know I can't make more money anywhere else or get twenty-five paid holidays—"

Monty interrupted her. "We're actually adding a twenty-sixth starting next year. We voted to make Tap Dance Day an official holiday. No one was getting any work done, anyway."

"That's great, but I'm sorry, my decision is still final. It's been a fun five years, but I have to go work somewhere else, anywhere else. Even if it's on an Alaskan fishing boat."

"You lack the constitution of a fisherman, Jane. I hear your issues though, and in anticipation of this meeting, I have already corrected them. This season, I'm taking the money we would have spent on your raise, or another very thoughtful and customized gift like the one that is apparently now destroyed, and we're instead giving you an underling."

Jane was confused. "You mean an employee? I'd be a supervisor?"

"Yes, and they would work with you on the seventh floor of the main building."

"I've been asking for that for years, Monty! You always said working in pairs doesn't tend to end well. What changed your mind? Why now?"

"You are very important to this company, Jane, and to our department especially. When you asked for the transfer to marketing at your last quarterly review, I almost literally died. In fact, I was legally dead for a full three minutes. I brought something back with me. It works in accounting."

Jane nodded, having met Loryn, who had processed her travel receipts.

"If you'll agree to stay another quarter, we will have your new employee, assistant to the manager of the Northwestern Inhuman Resources, in the office by tomorrow morning."

"And if I'm still not happy after next quarter, we can reassess my transfer request?" This was the part where she normally would cave, but today she wanted to play hardball.

Monty clutched his chest momentarily. Jane was torn between not wanting to see him die and a desire to gain another coworker as efficient as Loryn. He took a couple of slow deep gasps and seemed to steady himself.

"We can discuss the possibility of a transfer, but I guarantee we won't need to. You're going to love the person I hired. He reminds me a lot of you. Smart, efficient, sparkly, very much not on fire. You two will get along great." He rose from his seat and offered his hand. "Do we have a deal?"

Jane pretended to turn the idea over in her head, even though she had very much already made a decision. "We do," she said and shook his hand. As she did, he transformed into a sloth, and they were back on the trampoline, slowly bouncing up and down. The meeting was officially concluded, and she was once again still an employee of

Mystichem. This time, though, she had real hope that she might find a reason to stay that way forever!

★ ✱
★ ✶

Jane prepared the office as best she could for her new employee. She wiped down most of the surfaces she thought her employee would touch first so they wouldn't discover the inherent dampness right away. She stuffed the ceiling tiles with the howler monkey's favorite treat (SlimFast) laced with an over-the-counter medication that makes dogs drowsy. She had a long talk with the light switches about remaining on for most of the day, even if they felt she blinked for an excessive amount of time. It was unclear if they understood, but Jane felt confident as she stood before the elevator doors at 8:45 a.m.

At 8:55 a.m., exactly five minutes early (the perfect time to arrive in Jane's opinion), the elevator dinged and the doors slid open to reveal Mason. He was nothing like Jane had expected. When Monty said he reminded him of Jane, she had imagined someone similar in looks to her as well as personality—even though she was well aware that Mason could have been a robot, or a duck, or a ball of twine. There was a fantastic ball of twine running the PR department.

Mason was petite and blond with green eyes, where Jane was nearly six feet tall with very dark black skin and light brown eyes. She had to admit there was something in his posture, an efficiency of stance that reminded Jane of herself that first day on the job.

Jane extended her hand downward to shake. "Welcome to Mystichem!" she said.

Mason shook her hand enthusiastically and introduced himself. Jane offered to show him to his desk, which was very easy because the entire floor was empty but for two identical desks facing each other. Mason's desk had been there when Jane arrived at work that morning. It was completely set up already with a computer, office supplies, and framed pictures of a happy family, though it was unclear whose family it was.

Jane then offered to show Mason around the rest of the

Mystichem building. They started in the museum down in the basement, where a video wall told the story of how Mystichem started out as the world's leading manufacturer of collectable professional wrestling figurines and moved on to build an empire. They now manufactured and innovated in the fields of eating utensils, car batteries, water, hot plates, scary noises, birthday clowns, incurable diseases, gas station snacks, techno music, edible washing machines, drugs, helicopters, and many industries that they couldn't legally disclose. They had branches all over the country, but their pride and joy was their 155-story corporate office building.

They moved on to the cafeteria, the gym, the mail room, the screaming floor, the forbidden floor, the arcade, and the conference rooms. Mason showed special interest in the conference rooms, but sadly Jane had to tell him that Inhuman Resources rarely saw the need to use them since their team conferences were held in dreams and there was plenty of space on their floor for any interdepartmental meetings they had to host.

Next, Jane sat him down to explain some of the finer points of his job. "So, we are the only point of contact for the Inhuman Resources department for this entire building. Because the company is so big and retains such a diverse employee population, we have representatives for different groups of employees all over the place. Each group has their own special needs and accommodations. For instance, our vampire employees can obviously only work the night shift, so their Inhuman Resources rep works evenings as well. He also never eats garlic."

Mason nodded. "Yes, I understand. I have a background in Inhuman Resources. I realize Monty probably didn't tell you this, as it's bad luck for the supervisor to know anything about the employee before they begin working together."

"Oh, that's good to hear! But let me tell you what's different about working in this particular building. Most representatives service only one group, but we service all the people in this building, as well as the extremely volatile group of dragons who work in the mountains behind the main building for obvious space-related reasons. This means that occasionally . . ."

She paused and then corrected herself, not wanting to lie. "Often, we're called upon to settle disputes between various Inhumans." She pulled up a case file on her computer to show Mason. "For example, here is an ongoing case I've been dealing with. Each floor of the building is separated by department. The 6th floor is all accounting, the 155th floor is the CEO, the 153rd floor the CEO's shoe closet, and so forth

"The 83rd floor is procurement, and it recently welcomed a new junior procurement officer who transferred in from Scotland, David. He happens to be a sea monster, so naturally we flooded the entire floor with seawater. Grynold the Mystikal is a wizard and a coworker of David's. He would prefer that the floor not be flooded with seawater, as he prefers to breath air. This has caused a conflict between the two, and it's up to me—well, now us!—to mediate the conflict. In this case, we made a deal that the floor would be how David likes it Monday, Tuesday, and half of Wednesday, and how Grynold the Mystikal likes it the rest of the week. Both beings seemed to come away happy with the deal, but someone is still cursing their bathroom to contain only one square of toilet paper at all times. Therefore, the case is ongoing."

"Very interesting!" Mason replied.

He took copious notes, and in the following weeks he excelled at his job, going above and beyond the call of duty. He got the perverted ghost haunting the 22nd-floor bathroom to seek counseling. He negotiated a better deal on dental insurance for the mountain dragons, which was great because they all needed to have their wisdom teeth removed before they turned five hundred and the surgery became risky. He found a way to ship seventy-five W-2s to the core of the earth (or as the company called it, the negative 137th floor).

Jane was so happy.

Happy with his work ethic, at least, but socially they weren't really clicking. He was a big sports fan, and Jane was more of a Netflix-in-her-sloth-pajamas kind of girl. She liked comedies and he preferred action movies. Plus, he was secretive. He seemed reluctant to tell her even the most basic details about himself. She had to sneak a peek at his personnel file just to learn his middle name! It wasn't even an embarrassing name; it was Ferp. There were ten Ferps in security, though to be fair, they were all clones.

So, Jane's dissatisfaction and loneliness in her job continued.

One day, she came into the office early to find Mason already there, typing away on his computer. She greeted him and settled into her desk for the day, when a cold chill ran down her spine. Something was very, very wrong.

"Mason, do you hear that?" she asked.

He looked up from his desk, perplexed. "I don't hear anything."

"Exactly, it's 9 a.m. These are prime howling hours." She stood on her desk chair and lifted a ceiling tile, to find several tiny musical instruments. There were a couple of trumpets and some maracas, a Spanish guitar, and a violin. Each had a tiny bottle of SlimFast duct-taped to it. Mason was grinning from ear to ear when she glanced down at him.

"I got rid of the monkeys," he said.

Jane got down from her chair slowly. "How?" she asked. "I've been petitioning the building to remove them for years."

"I got the idea from you, actually. I saw the one you put in a tattered little mariachi outfit. He was using my computer when I came back up after visiting the gym one night. It's troubling how smart those monkeys were getting. I think they might have been trying to steal my identity. Anyway, you can't remove an endangered species from its natural habitat, but it's also illegal for a mariachi band to inhabit the building. So I wrestled them all into little outfits and got them to hold the instruments. Then I reported them to security, and they took care of the rest."

"You're a genius, Mason," Jane said with her mouth, but it wasn't how she felt in her heart. She had actually gotten pretty used to the howler monkeys and wished a little bit that she had gotten to say goodbye.

"No problem," Mason replied with a grin slightly too large for his mouth. "We should get ready for the big staff meeting tomorrow. I'm so excited to finally meet the team. Oh, that reminds me; someone named The World Eater called and left a message asking me to disentomb him for the meeting?"

"No!" Jane quickly replied.

"That's what I figured." He crumpled up the piece of paper he had written the message on and threw it in the wastebasket.

The lights took that moment as the perfect opportunity to turn off. Jane sighed and slipped on her night vision goggles.

Mason fumbled around his desk in the darkness. "Hey, have you heard back from procurement about my night vision goggles?"

"They promised me they were working on it," Jane assured him. "At least, I think that's what three flags means. I really wish they would use something other than a maritime communication system."

That night, she appeared in her coworker Helen's dream, along with Monty, The World Eater, Bubba, and Uncool Helen. Helen was boxing a tyrannosaurus and winning handily due to its very short arms. Monty shooed the T. rex away and surveyed the gathered group.

"Looks like just about everyone is here, except for Mason. Jane, where is your employee?"

"I'm not sure," Jane replied honestly.

"Hm, he must be having a pretty intense dream. I hate those. He might be crying. You go and get him, Jane. Everyone else, let's pull some folding chairs into the ring and get started with old business."

Jane meant to protest, but she found herself standing in a burnt field. The air didn't smell like smoke or grass, though, as if the field had been burned a long time ago and never recovered. The smell left behind had a metallic quality to it that was blown into her nostrils by a harsh, dry wind. The sky was red. Her footsteps crunched as she walked through the desolate landscape. Mason was nowhere in sight.

She walked for quite a while in the flat burnt land, until she came upon a slight hill. Just over the top of it, she could see Mason.

He was gigantic, the size of a skyscraper. His low maniacal laugh rumbled across the barren field. People started pouring over the edge of the hill. They were running from him. He reached out with gigantic greedy hands and grabbed one of the runners. It was a black girl in a gray business suit, her natural hair was styled in a tight bun, the way Jane often did hers.

That's when Jane realized it *was* her!

The other people running over the hill had reached her now. A man in a tan suit jostled her, causing him to drop his briefcase.

"Apologies," he said formally as he bent to retrieve it. It was Monty!

Jane grabbed his shoulders. "Monty, what's going on here?" she asked.

"Hm, looks like I'm not really Monty, but a dreamed reflection of Monty created by someone else. If I were the real Monty, I would pop that guy like a small child's balloon. As is, it looks like I'm running, and you probably should too. He really doesn't like you."

"Smash, smash, smash, Jane!" Mason bellowed. As he did, he squeezed his fist and brought his free hand down on the dream version of Jane's head. Jane gasped, and his eyes shot up. He looked right at her.

She stumbled backward, right into a folding chair. She was in the boxing ring again. Mason sat beside her with his usual friendly smile painted on.

"Welcome, Mason and Jane. So glad you two could make it. Everybody, please welcome our newest team member, Mason Whittick." There was polite applause from everyone who had hands.

"Let's go ahead and continue with old business. We were just discussing cost-cutting measures. Uncool Helen has suggested downgrading the ferns in the lobby from evil to just plain menacing."

"Boo!" Helen cried.

"Hiss," agreed The World Eater.

No one seemed to notice how tightly Jane was gripping the seat of her chair.

Since she wasn't the type of person who let things simmer, Jane decided to confront Mason first thing the next morning at work. She went in early, and the lights were off. They tended to dislike turning on before 8 a.m. She was surprised to make out through the darkness Mason sitting at *her* desk with his feet up and wearing *her* night vision goggles. Fortunately, she had very good eyesight, or she might not have known how offended she should be.

"What are you doing at my desk?" Jane gasped.

"I'm just getting comfortable, Jane," Mason snarled. "I figure there's no need to hide my true form from you anymore." He reached into his pocket and pulled out a small stick-on mustache with curled ends. It looked fantastic on him.

Instantly, Jane understood that while in most cases mustaches were neutral and only became good or bad based on the wearer, this mustache was meant to represent that he was evil. "Evil people aren't allowed to work at Mystichem unless their evilness is clearly disclosed pre-employment!" Jane said.

"Oh, Monty knows I'm evil," Mason replied.

Jane gasped. "Really?"

"No, I lied because I'm evil." Mason threw his head back and let out an evil laugh that echoed through the room.

It was so loud, it startled the lights into turning on.

He yelled and pulled off the night vision goggles, rubbing his eyes vigorously. "I'm after your job, Jane, and I'm not even going to hide it anymore. I'm going to take this big, juicy job right out from under your nose, and there's nothing you can do to stop me!"

"That's all you want? My job?"

"Yes."

"You can have it."

Mason looked very uncertain. "Really? Wait, I want something else too."

"What?"

"This mechanical pencil."

"Part pencil, part machine, all efficiency. Nice choice, you can have it."

"No foolin'?"

"None at all. I just want this picture of a happy family and my Ruth Bader Ginsburg figurine, and I'm good to go. I'll turn my resignation in to you right now. You'll just have to tell Monty for me." Jane beamed, having finally found a way out of her terrible job. She waved to Mason as the elevator doors slid shut.

"Wait!" he called after her. "Show me how to work the projector one more time."

The doors closed, and she sank further and further away from the seventh floor at a rapid pace.

That afternoon, she went to a local bookstore / coffee shop and enjoyed an extra sugary latte and a romance novel in a big, soft armchair. She stayed at the bookstore so long that she eventually struck up a conversation with an employee and found out they were hiring.

By that evening, she had a new job. Her new job was silent and smelled like coffee instead of mold, and the lights turned on and off exactly when you asked them to, and it was only damp in places where it made sense to be damp.

And Jane was miserable.

That night, she dreamed of running down a long, dry road with nothing in front of or behind her, just miles and miles of empty road. Soon, she heard footsteps beside her and turned to see Monty, still in his suit and tie, keeping pace with her.

"Hello, Jane. I just have some paperwork for you to sign." He pulled out a pen and a thick bundle of documents.

Jane stopped running. Finding herself suddenly winded, she doubled over to catch her breath. She took the documents, and Monty turned around and offered his back. She started to sign but then reconsidered.

"I should probably read through these real quick," she said.

"Of course." He turned around to stare at her as she read through the standard NDA, memory erasure, and donated-organ return paperwork.

She glanced away and ended up looking at the vast empty space behind her, and ahead. "I'm worried that I'll never be happy, Monty," she said.

Monty thought this over for a moment. "I don't think I'm a great person to talk to about that, Jane. Mostly because I'm not an actual person, I'm a physical manifestation of the concept of management. All the Mystichem managers are."

Jane nodded.

"I will say that it seems to me you have put an awful lot of blame on your work for making you unhappy, and I have done everything I can to fix that for you, but you've never really elaborated on what makes you unhappy. You said you were lonely, so I got you a coworker, and he reported that you two didn't get along."

"It was a bad match. He's evil."

"That may be true, but even so, what else could be changed about the job to make you happy? You seem to like helping people and doing paperwork and negotiating, all things you get to do every day. What job do you think will make you happy?"

There wasn't a single thing that came to Jane's mind. "Maybe my job wasn't making me unhappy. Maybe I'm unhappy because I'm unhappy."

"It seems to me, in my interactions with my underlings, that not everyone gains fulfillment from their work. There are many other ways to be fulfilled. When I clock out at the end of the day, I simply cease to exist, but I know Uncool Helen is the captain of her roller hockey team. Bubba volunteers at a shelter for abandoned puzzle pieces. The World Eater knits. These are all things other than work that bring them joy. Although to me that is a ridiculous concept, perhaps there's an apt lesson in that for you?"

"I don't know why I'm unhappy, and it might take me a while to figure out exactly what it is, but I do know one thing. I don't want to quit my job."

"I'm sorry, Jane, but you've already quit your job, as promised."

"Promised to who?"

"No one. Never mind. I'm sorry, but I'm afraid while you were talking, you seemed to have signed the paperwork." She looked down to see that this was true, she had been signing her name without even realizing it as she and Monty spoke.

"You are no longer an employee of Mystichem. Your organs will be returned to you at our earliest convenience. Have a nice life."

Jane had said that sentence to so many people in the past, but it felt bizarre and wrong to have it said to her. "Monty, please wait!" she called, but he had already disappeared.

The next day, Jane woke up with a monkey on her back—a howler monkey in a torn mariachi outfit. It was Robert! "Good morning, sleeping beauty," he said.

Jane had many questions. "Robert, you're here? You can talk? You have a British accent?"

"Of course I can talk, but I prefer howling, don't you? It's so much more expressive."

"Not really," Jane admitted. She rolled over slowly and sat up. "What are you doing here?" she asked.

"I've escaped those uncultured dilettantes at the Brookfield Zoo to warn you that Mason is evil!"

"I know, he showed me his mustache."

"It looks fabulous on him, doesn't it?"

"It does," she replied, although she hated to admit it.

"Oh, good, so you know he's planning to bring down the company. It seems I knifed that zoo security officer for no reason."

"Bring down the company? I thought he just wanted to steal my job?"

"No! That was just the first step in his evil plan."

"What's he going to do next?"

"Do you happen to have any SlimFast?" Robert asked, not at all slyly.

Jane didn't have any on her. Luckily, she lived just down the street from a supermarket. She put a hat and sunglasses on Robert after he convinced her that special operatives from the zoo were looking for him.

Once they had retrieved the SlimFast and gotten back in the car, Jane popped open a bottle and handed it to him.

"Spill," she said.

Robert took a long pull from the bottle. "The night he got us kicked out of the building, out of our home. I'll never forget it. It was the worst night of my life—the grabbing and the cursing and the howling, which was lovely, but the rest of it was awful. I was using Mason's computer to catfish Magik: The Gathering players into buying me SlimFast, when an email alert popped up. I'm a naturally curious animal, so I opened it. Remember that deal he brokered for the dragons' health insurance? The one that seemed too good to be true?"

Jane leaned in intently. "Yes?"

"Well, it was! He forged the paperwork, and now every dragon in the company is being sent claim denials for their wisdom teeth surgeries."

"No!"

"Yes, and that's a ten-thousand-dollar surgery. It requires three dentists just to lift a tooth."

"The dragons will be furious."

Robert nodded in agreement. "And who do you think they'll blame?"

"Mystichem! Dragons are so temperamental anyway, and they're probably still in pain from the surgery. They're bound to lash out at the company."

"Now you're getting it. Mason discovered that I knew his plan, and he was furious. He already had those mariachi outfits in his desk in case we ever crossed him, but I had no idea. He chased us down and forced every last one of us into the costumes. When the security guards arrived, I tried to reason with them. I said, 'Ferp, you know me, man. Have you ever seen me play mariachi music before?' But he wouldn't listen. I think Mason's got them in his pocket. They dragged us out of there like we were dogs, not monkeys."

A knock on the window made them both jump. There was a man in a zoo security uniform.

Robert pulled out a switchblade. "I'll cut my way out of this, I swear to God," he screeched. He whipped his tail around and broke the back driver-side window, quickly maneuvering out of it. "Hurry,

Jane!" he yelled as he ran away. "You won't have much time. He'll know I've escaped and that I'd go straight to you."

The zoo security guard gave chase.

Jane didn't hesitate. Hitting the accelerator, she headed straight for Mystichem. It wasn't until she reached the front door that she realized her badge had been deactivated and she could no longer access the building. This momentarily stalled her heroic dash for the building with no plan. Honestly, she felt like she didn't need a plan. She could defeat Mason with the sheer force of being very good at her job. It didn't make any sense at all, but it was also just crazy enough to work.

She burst into the lobby. One of the Ferps was behind the check-in desk. She took a deep breath, slid off her heels, and sprinted right past him. He gave chase, catching up to her at the elevator banks, where the chase had to abruptly stop.

"I'm sorry, Jane, but Mr. Whittock has instructed us not to let you back into the building as you've been terminated."

"I was not terminated. I quit! And I just need to get to my computer so I can fix the mess that Mason has made. If I don't, there could be rampaging dragons headed here any minute." She mashed the elevator button as quickly as she could as she spoke.

Ferp stalked toward her slowly, carefully skirting the reach of the lobby ferns as he did so.

The elevator dinged. "I'm sorry, ma'am, but for the safety of the company, I'm not going to be able to let you go through those doors." He moved more quickly toward her.

"I'm sorry, but for the safety of the company, I'm going to have to do this." She reared back and kicked Ferp as hard as she could, straight into the fern. It wrapped its leaves around his neck and began to strangle him. Thank God they had voted against downgrading them to menacing.

Mason wasn't expecting her when she arrived at the seventh floor, which was evident because he wasn't wearing the mustache. As soon as he saw her, he ran to his desk to retrieve it.

"Stop right there!" Jane commanded.

To her surprise, Mason stopped. "It doesn't matter now, Jane. I'm assuming Robert's paid you a little visit? Well, the damage has already been done, so what are you going to do now?"

"I'm . . . I'm going to call Red Pentagram Red Arrow and negotiate with them for coverage."

Mason threw his head back and cackled his signature evil laugh. "Even if you still worked here, you'd have to be the best negotiator in the world to make that deal."

"Watch me," Jane replied, lunging for her desk.

Mason darted toward her, but he slipped on a patch of excessively damp floor. Jane shuffled past him. Just as he reached for her leg, the lights decided to turn off. He missed her by just a few inches, close enough that she felt the air around her disturbed. Quicker than she had ever moved before in her life, she snatched Mason's phone off his desk and darted into the bathroom, locking the door behind her.

Mason pounded on the door as she dialed Red Pentagram Red Arrow. "I'll just unplug the phone cord, Jane," he bellowed.

Jane knew this was where she could use her superior knowledge of the Mystichem facilities to defeat him. Unfortunately, there was absolutely nothing relevant she could think of to help her at that particular juncture, so she decided to use the fact that she was a very good liar in times of crisis to defeat him.

"You can unplug the phone from the wall if you want, Mason," she replied.

"I can?"

"Yes, but it will trigger one of the many fine ancient Sumerian death curses attached to our office equipment."

Mason was silent.

"Hi, can I speak with Keesha? This is Jane from Mystichem," she whispered into the receiver.

She was quickly transferred to Keesha. "Jane! I thought Mason said you weren't with the company anymore."

Mason continued to pound on the door, but thankfully he had abandoned the unplugging the phone cord plan, apparently unwilling to test out Jane's death curse bluff after what had happened when he used the stapler improperly. There really were a lot of cursed office supplies. The phone just happened not to be one of them.

"Just a little misunderstanding," Jane replied. "I was just calling to speak with you about another little mix-up: the dragons' dental insurance."

After about ten minutes of working over Mason's screeching threats (luckily, Keesha was used to hearing strange sounds while they spoke on the phone), they had reached a deal that would involve the company covering a portion of the expenses themselves, but it was ultimately better than being attacked by a rage of dragons in post-dental surgery pain.

Just as they were saying their goodbyes, the lock finally gave and Mason burst in. He was wearing the night vision goggles. Jane was sitting on the floor of the stall, and he grabbed her by her ankles to drag her out.

"Say hi to the kids for me!" she yelled as he dragged her out from under the door. He and Jane wrestled with the receiver.

They could hear Keesha on the other end saying, "Jeremy's taken up piano."

Mason tried to rip the phone from her hands. Just as her grip began to give, the lights popped back on again, blinding Mason. He shouted and pulled off the goggles. Jane scrambled from underneath him, hung up the phone, and darted to the elevator, but three of the Ferps were already there, waiting for her. One of them had an extremely irritated neck.

"I'm allergic to ferns," he said angrily as they each grabbed an arm.

Jane looked helplessly on as Mason waved goodbye to her with the phone receiver. He was going to undo all the good work she had done.

"Where are you taking me?" she asked the Ferp on her left.

"You don't . . ." said the the Ferp on her left.

"Ask questions," the Ferp on her right finished.

They took her to the 154th floor. She had never been up this high before. They marched her down a long white hallway and heaved her into an all-white room with a comfortable single bed, locking the door with a final-sounding click.

"Where are you going?" Jane yelled, her face pressed against the metal door. "You can't just leave me here!"

No one answered.

Jane perched on the bed and waited. How long would they leave her here? Hours? Days? What would they do to her? She had heard rumors of bad employees who disappeared and were never heard from again. Or worse, who reappeared as morning show hosts on local television stations. Would they turn her over to the police? Would they hurt her? Only time would tell.

One of the Ferps returned with a strange machine. She hugged her knees to her chest as he plugged it into the wall and pushed a button. The sound of crashing ocean waves filled the room.

"Do you prefer ocean or rainforest?" he asked.

"Ocean's fine, I suppose," Jane replied.

"Good. Do you need any warm milk?"

"Um, no. I'm fine, thank you."

"Good. Now go to sleep, or else. You've got a very important meeting."

She thought it might be difficult to take a nap so early in the morning but soon found the soothing sound of the waves dragging her off to sleep. Her dream was like a movie. She dreamed of Robert's warning and Mason's mustache. When she got to the part where the guards captured her, she found herself sitting in a lavish office with plush green carpeting and soft leather furniture. A man in a tan suit holding a briefcase looked out the floor-to-ceiling windows that displayed the Chicago skyline.

"Monty?" It certainly looked like him.

He turned around and smiled at her. "Hello, Jane. Thank you for joining me. I'm not your supervisor. My name is Jack. I'm the CEO of Mystichem.

"I'm sorry my office is so difficult to get to, but now that I've seen what happened, I wanted to speak to you in person. To thank you, of course."

Jane exhaled a sigh of relief, certain both that she had saved the company and would not be forced to host a daytime television show.

Jack sat down next to her in a leather chair. "You have prevented a major disaster within our company, and we are very grateful. You've made Monty very proud. You've made all of us physical embodiments of the concept of management very proud."

"Thank you," Jane replied.

"I hope that your returning here, kicking one of our security guards, assaulting your former coworker, and rescuing us all from being eaten by angry dragons is a sign that you would like to return to your old position?"

"Yes, very much, sir."

"Fantastic."

"What about Mason, sir? Will he be punished?"

"Oh, he'll be fine. I'm sure he'll love the morning show we're arranging for him. It has an entire segment devoted to silly hats." He grinned devilishly.

Jane woke up to find the door to the white room unlocked. She escorted herself into the elevator and back down to the seventh floor. It was the worst floor in the entire building, possibly one of the worst places in the entire world—no, the entire universe—but as she stepped back into it, Jane felt happy.

Happily?

Adam Carlson

Once upon a time, there was a prince who set off on a quest to find a princess to wed, although he did not relish the idea of slaying dragons. Or rescuing damsels in distress. The thought of performing herculean tasks made him slightly queasy. All things considered, he would have rather been vacationing on a tropical island than trekking cross-country.

He lost his way and wandered through the woods until he came to a tower that meandered skyward, looking like it could have done with the use of a plumb line during construction. The prince circumnavigated the shrubs and weeds that had overgrown the base of the edifice, looking for an entrance that would hopefully provide access to a warm bath and a cup of tea in addition to shelter.

After one circuit, he sputtered. "There's no door here!"

"What's that?" someone called from above. "Is someone down there?" It was a lovely voice, of a timbre that made one expect that the owner had more beauty than she knew what to do with.

The prince tilted back his head and saw a woman peering down from a window at the top of the tower. "I am Prince Eric," he called, "and I was hoping to have a bit of rest."

"You've come to save me?"

"Um . . . you need to be saved?"

"I am Rapunzel," the lady called. "I've been locked in this tower by an evil witch!" She disappeared, and a pile of string tumbled out the window and plopped to the ground, leaving a sort of rope up to the top. "Climb up, and you may help me escape from her clutches!"

"Climb?" Prince Eric poked at the faux ladder. "That sounds rather difficult."

"Don't worry; my hair is strong. It will hold you."

"That's your hair?"

"Of course."

The prince gave the blonde strands a suspicious glance and wiped his hand on his tunic. He didn't want to touch the hair again if he didn't have to. "Have you washed this recently?"

"What?"

"It just seems a bit unsanitary. And an awful lot of work. It would be much easier if there were a different way to get in."

"There aren't any stairs."

"Oh, good gracious, I don't think I could climb that many stairs. I'd be winded halfway up. Now, if there were some sort of motorized contraption that could lift me up and down . . ."

"If I had something like that, I wouldn't need to be rescued, would I?" the prisoner retorted.

"I suppose not." The prince scratched his head. His father expected him to rescue a girl, and this damsel in distress might be perfect if it weren't so difficult to get to her. Just because he had to perform a heroic act didn't mean he had to put in a lot of effort, did it? Besides, there was a wicked witch who would probably be upset if he rescued her, and Prince Eric definitely didn't want to deal with that kind of baggage.

The prince walked away. When Rapunzel called out "Are you going to rescue me or not?" he didn't even pause to respond.

Not far away, a princess wandered through the marshes, somehow stumbling through the muck without besmirching her white dress.

"I can't believe this!" she griped.

"Can't believe what?" a voice croaked.

"Who said that?"

A large, grotesque frog leaped onto a log in front of her. "I did," it croaked.

The princess shrieked with as much dignity as she could. "Get away!" she cried.

"I just asked a question. Why are you so upset?"

"Why am I so upset? Just look at me! My father thinks that for me to get married I have to be rescued by a brave prince, so he sent me away to be captured by an ogre or imprisoned by a wizard or something. Now, I'm in the middle of nowhere, trying to keep out of this grime and talking to a misshapen toad."

"I'm a frog."

"You're gross, is what you are. Now get away."

"I'm a prince."

"Very funny."

"I'm serious. I was cursed by a wizard. I'm waiting to be turned back into my true form."

The princess leaned in a little closer and inspected the dark green skin and buggy yellow eyes. "Suppose I believe you. What would I have to do to turn you back?"

"Kiss me."

"Disgusting."

"It would only take a moment."

"I don't kiss things that have scales."

"Frogs don't have scales."

"I barely kiss things that have skin."

The frog did its best imitation of a shrug. "It would get you out of the swamp."

The princess thought it over and began to lean in, despite the creature's sliminess. She was inches away when she saw a large purple pustule on the frog's backside. She stood abruptly and cried, "Hideous!"

Before the frog could protest, another voice called, "Who the devil put all this mud here?" Prince Eric emerged from the foliage, trying to beat mosquitoes away with his sword.

"Who are you?" the princess demanded.

"Prince Eric. Who are you?"

"Princess Gladwin." She glanced at the frog, then back at Eric. "I need to be rescued."

Eric looked around. "From what?"

"This frog."

"That's ridiculous," the frog said.

Eric considered the situation for a moment. Rescuing this princess from a small frog was certainly easier than climbing a tower. "Okay. Come on, then."

The princess tiptoed after him as he led her toward civilization.

"Wait, you can't go!" the frog called after them. "She's supposed to kiss me!"

"Get a different princess," Gladwin called over her shoulder.

"But . . . but . . ."

Eric paused long enough to point back the way he'd come. "There was a girl trapped in a tower back there." Then the newly united couple was out of sight, heading on their way to a new life and leaving the frog alone.

Rapunzel had wept when Eric left. She supposed it was pointless; what's the use in crying over someone who is so obviously inept? And yet there she was, still stuck in her tower with no rescue in sight.

"Excuse me," a voice called, breaking her out of her reverie, "but is there a young woman trapped up there?"

"Yes!" Rapunzel dashed to the window and looked down, but she didn't see anyone. "Have you come to rescue me?"

"Um, I think so," the voice said. "As soon as I figure out how to do it."

"Come out and I will help you up."

"I'm right here."

This confused the girl, but she strained her eyes in case she'd somehow missed a person standing in the open. "I don't see you."

A small speck of green dislodged itself from the swath of grass and hopped around a bit. "See?"

"Are you a grasshopper?"

"I'm a frog."

"Oh." Rapunzel thought about this a bit. "Well, I was sort of expecting a human."

"I'm actually a prince who's been cursed."

Rapunzel smiled. "That's all right, then. I'll just lower my hair, and you can rescue me." She picked up the mass of strands and tossed it out. The frog barely got out of the way before the end crashed into the ground. "Climb up!" she called to him.

"Can't you come down here, instead?"

"If I could get down there by myself, I wouldn't need to be rescued, would I?"

He looked doubtfully at the makeshift rope. "I don't think this is going to work."

She sighed. "You think it's too difficult too?"

"Well, it's not that it's just difficult. It's impossible."

"What is it with all you princes and knights who can't seem to find the strength to climb a tower? What's wrong with you?"

"I can't exactly climb." The frog held up his hands. "No opposable thumbs."

"Oh." Rapunzel slumped against the wall, trying not to cry. "I suppose that's the best excuse I've heard so far."

"Don't get me wrong; I'm not giving up!"

"You're not?"

"I mean, well . . . you will kiss me if I rescue you, right?"

"I'd kiss a famished tiger if it rescued me."

"I'll take that as a yes. Now, I just have to figure out how to get up there."

"You don't have hands, but could you hold on with something else?"

The frog croaked with joy. He flicked out his tongue and wrapped it around a few strands of the hair. "Gwoth," he mumbled around his tongue. "Okay, I'b weady! Pull be up!"

The hair rose slowly as Rapunzel hauled it in, and the plan might have worked if she had taken better care of her hair. Unfortunately, the constant rubbing against the stone windowsill had made her hair weak, and the few strands that the frog held onto broke free when he was less than halfway up. He plummeted into the weeds and bounced away from the building.

"Are you okay?" Rapunzel cried.

The frog groaned. "Yes."

"Do you want to try again?"

"Um, I think that I'll find some other way to get up there," he said. "I'll be back."

Meanwhile, Prince Eric and Princess Gladwin had made it out of the wilderness and found a road.

Gladwin bemoaned the dreadful state of her clothing and hair. "I don't see why you wouldn't carry me through the woods."

"Because you're heavy," muttered the prince.

"What?"

"Nothing."

"I'll never be able to get this dress clean again. And I've got a twig in my hair! A twig!"

"Where is your kingdom?"

The princess looked around to get her bearings. "About ten days' journey that way." She pointed.

Eric considered it, then turned in the opposite direction. "My kingdom is only about a two-day journey this way."

Gladwin stared at him. "You expect me to go to your terrible little country just because it's closer?"

Eric shrugged. "It would be easier."

Gladwin rolled her eyes. "Oh, I suppose. I wouldn't want my parents to see me in this awful state, anyway."

They trudged slowly down the road.

* *
* *

The frog returned two days later, pulling a cart with a fancy contraption on it.

"I was worried you weren't going to come," Rapunzel admitted.

"You couldn't pay me to stay away," the frog replied.

"What did you bring?"

The frog hopped into a small sling. "It's a trebuchet."

"What's that?"

"The man who built it assured me that it would get me into that tower." The frog pulled a small cord, releasing the swinging arm of the device. The counterweight dropped, the plank of wood rotated, and the sling whipped around, sending the flailing amphibian directly into the wall ten feet below the window. He bounced off and fell into the weeds below.

"Did that hurt?"

"No, it's fine." The frog groaned. "I'm squishy."

"I don't know if you want to try it, but I made a basket for you to ride in. I'll tie it to the end of a braid and pull you up. That way, you won't have to hold on at all, and my hair won't break."

"Brilliant!"

She lowered a basket made of dead leaves and small twigs at the end of a golden braid until it gently touched the ground.

"Are you sure this will work?" the frog asked. "It doesn't look particularly sturdy."

"If the witch let me keep things to build with, I would have escaped a long time ago," Rapunzel explained. "Most of it, I stole from the birds' nests up here."

"Did you say that there's a witch involved in this scenario?"

"Oh, yes. Did I forget to mention that?" Rapunzel grimaced with concern. "That isn't a deal breaker, is it? I mean, you won't run away just because of some witch, will you?"

"I've already got a wizard who's angry at me. What's one magical villain more or less?" He hopped into the basket with great aplomb. Rapunzel grinned ear to ear as she hauled her hair up . . . and left the bottom of the basket on the ground.

"Sorry, but it looks like I'm a bit too heavy for this," the frog said. "Don't worry; I've got another idea."

He hopped away while Rapunzel gazed wistfully after him.

Eric and Gladwin had arrived in his kingdom, and the princess was not taking it very well. "You call this dump a castle?" she demanded.

"I always thought it was a good one."

"If you expect me to sit around in this stink hole, you'd better add an expansion."

"That sounds like a lot of work."

"That's what your servants are for. And you call this a moat? It's a ditch, at best. And get those dreary tapestries off the walls. I'll decorate this place with a proper woman's touch. We'll have this place shipshape in the next week, or I'll be leaving."

Eric was just considering if it might not be easier all around to just let her leave when a servant came bustling into the room. "Your Majesty!" he cried. "We just heard that you had returned. Thank goodness you are here! We are being attacked by the kingdom to the north!"

"What do they want?" Eric asked.

"There's nothing here worth taking," Gladwin added.

"They'll take the castle," the servant said. "And all the land. Sire, you must lead our army against them."

"Must I?" Prince Eric asked.

Rapunzel was tired of waiting around, so she made her own desperate attempt at escape. Knowing her hair was in disrepair, she braided it as tightly as she could to give it more strength and then tied the end to the rafters. Slowly, cautiously, she rappelled down the side of the tower. She expected the look on the frog's face would be priceless when he found her waiting patiently at the bottom, and she thought the look on his face after she kissed him would be even better.

Unfortunately, her plans hitched on a minor snag when she reached the end of her hair before the bottom of the tower. For safety, she had tied her hair to the strongest rafter, which proved to be about ten feet too far from the window.

Hanging by her head, she wondered how she could possibly get out of the predicament. It would have been much easier if she'd had any sort of sharp object, but she had to make do without. Reaching up, she began breaking the strands of her hair, one by one.

She was three quarters of the way through when the rest gave way. She banged and bounced along the wall until she landed in the grass. What remained of her hair was a disheveled mess with a patch of blood at the back, where some of the hair had pulled out at the roots.

"It'll grow back," she murmured to herself. She lay without moving, staring up at the tower. The exhilaration of freedom and the anticipation of uniting with her true love was beat out by the exhaustion of the escape.

And then, as she lay there, she saw a red kite that had lost its string, floating above. It had a strangely familiar green speck on it and seemed to fly determinedly toward the open window of the tower. It went in, and she heard a voice cry from above: "I've made it! Rapunzel, I am finally here! Where are you?"

"Oh, no," Rapunzel muttered, then yelled, "I'm down here!"

The green head peered out the window. "You escaped!"

"Yes, but now I can't get back up to you. I can't reach my hair to climb."

"Forget that. I'll jump."

"But—"

Rapunzel didn't have any more time to protest because the small green body hurtled itself into space. As he plummeted, she jumped to her feet and scrambled around to find where he would land.

He plopped into her open hands.

"You caught me," he said, somewhat surprised.

She smiled. "I'll never let you go."

"I can't believe you let them take your castle," Gladwin whined.

"We can always go to your kingdom," Eric said.

"You think I want my parents to meet you? What would I tell them? 'I got rescued by a slob of a prince, and now he doesn't have a kingdom, and he's an idiot'? I think not."

"Then what will we do?"

"You'll have to get another kingdom. A better one."

"That sounds like a lot of work."

As they meandered along the road, a young couple holding hands traipsed past them. The girl was blonde with a ragged haircut and a dress that was ripped and torn as if she'd been mountain climbing. The boy had an almost green complexion, wore an ill-fitting outfit, and was in desperate need of some grooming.

Gladwin looked after them with a haughty glare. "Disgusting."

"They looked happy," Eric said.

"Of course. They're both just odious enough for each other."

Eric sighed. "Yes. I suppose some people have it easy."

And they all lived . . . ever after.

About the Authors

Taylor Adel has a semi-concerning obsession with writing her own twisted tales and reading the fictional work of others. She spent half her childhood in the library with her mother and the other half at movie theaters with her father, so it's safe to say that storytelling is as intrinsic to her life as breathing.

She received her bachelor's degree in English with an emphasis in creative writing from Avila University, where she graduated cum laude. Now she is working toward her teaching certification while attending an MFA program. It is her dream to teach literature and creative writing at the collegiate level.

Her short stories have been published in multiple magazines, including *Five:2:One*, *Every Day Fiction*, the *Birmingham Arts Journal*, *All the Sins*, and more. She has finished her first short story collection and her first novel, an adult high fantasy called *Marked by Fire*.

Ed Ahern resumed writing after forty-odd years in foreign intelligence and international sales. He's had one hundred ninety poems and stories published so far, and three books. He works the other side of writing at Bewildering Stories, where he sits on the review board and manages a posse of five review editors.

Douglas Anstruther was raised among the long, cold winters of Minnesota. At age seven, he discovered that there were other worlds beyond our own and was astonished, and frankly disappointed, that no one had thought this important enough to mention earlier—a sentiment he still holds today. At some point, he married his lovely wife, Dana, went to medical school, had three very nearly perfect children, and moved to Wilmington, North Carolina. When not tending to people's kidneys, Douglas likes to read, write, and talk about history, linguistics, space, AIs, the singularity, and everything in between. He particularly enjoys writing stories that will rattle around in a reader's head for a while after the last page has been turned.

Lydia Bugg is a humor writer whose work has been featured on Cracked.com, BunnyEars.com, TheModernRogue.com, and more. She lives in Nashville, Tennessee, with her dog, Gravy, and her husband, Lucas. She just realized she is the one writing this bio and can put whatever she wants in it. Lydia Bugg is six foot five and can totally dunk a basketball. Her best friends are a talking unicorn, who sounds like the actress Jennifer Lawrence, and the actress Jennifer Lawrence. She has an Emmy and an Oscar, and she forces them to fight every night for money.

Adam Carlson is a stay-at-home dad who spends his idle time writing (mostly when the kids are napping). "PR" was the first story he has published, and it appeared in *Eclectically Heroic* last year. He looks forward to having more stories published soon.

Kelly Lynn Colby is a professional volunteer, fledgling writer, and hardcore geek. She volunteers with the Girl Scouts and Boy Scouts, as well as the high school her son attends and the farm where her daughter learns equestrian skills. She has joined Inklings Publishing as both an acquisitions editor and a developmental editor. Her epic fantasy, *Tarbin's True Heir*, was released in September 2017. When she is not attending to her myriad duties, Kelly enjoys reading and traveling, especially to sci-fi conventions, such as Dragon Con.

Kelsey Dean currently lives in Seoul, where she teaches English, writes, and paints. Her fiction and poetry have appeared or are forthcoming in a variety of publications, including *The Binge-Watching Cure*, *Cast of Wonders*, *Liminal Stories*, and *Cicada*. Her YA short story "Starfishing" is available on Audible.com, and she occasionally blogs at kelseypaints.tumblr.com.

Sir Andross Draneg was born on the planet Jorn in the city Dran on his father's prosperous farm. During the war before unification on Jorn, Andross proved himself such a worthy warrior that he was knighted. In service to King Amiel and Queen Verena, Sir Andross was often sent on a variety of missions. Thanks to these, he collected notebooks full of myths, legends, and other assorted tales from the peoples of Thyrein's Galactic Wall. Having found his journals, Fern Brady has taken it upon herself to bring these well-written stories to the readers of Earth.

Ashley Lynn Field enjoys her life as a professional dork, perpetual annoyance, and otherwise erratic laser beam in the eye of life. While not procrastinating to the full extent of her being, she can be found on Twitch cohosting Horseshoes and Hand Grenades, playing video games (poorly and with gusto), engaging in spirited bouts of Dungeons and Dragons, or fast asleep.

Kimberly Gail grew up in Kansas but has neither lived on a farm nor been swept away to a magical land by a tornado. She does, however, craft magical worlds in her mind that she lovingly transforms into words through her writing.

She is a mother of three: two newly minted adults and one highly opinionated preteen whom she is currently homeschooling.

You can find Kimberly at kimberlygail.com, where she shares about writing, life, parenthood, spirituality, and homeschool. You can also find her on Instagram at kimberly_gail_writers_life, as well as on Facebook.

Citlalin Ossio is a hungry panda who graduated from the University of Houston with a degree in Media Production in 2016. She was a 2017 Women in Horror Film Festival finalist for her screenplay adaptation of Meg Hafdahl's short story "Guts."

She is a Mexican American whose hours of playing video games, especially *Legend of Zelda* games, and watching anime and Korean dramas (which she justifies as "storytelling research") fueled her desire to write fantasies and rom-coms. She lives in Houston, Texas, and loves eating, being with her family, creating art in whatever medium, and plotting new ways to make the universe fall in love with pandas.

Dorothy Tinker grew up dreaming of fantastical worlds and creatures, of plots in space, and of strange new cultures. After studying mathematics in university, she rediscovered her true passion and rededicated herself to her literary dreams.

Since then, Dorothy has published an ongoing series of YA spiritual/fantasy novels, including *Peace of Evon*, *Gift of War*, and *Lost King*. Her short stories have been published in various anthologies by HWG Press, Inklings Publishing, Writespace, and Balance of Seven. Her poetry has been published in OWS's *Primal Elements*.

You can follow Dorothy on Facebook at @DorothyTinkerAuthor and on Twitter at @dorothy_tinker. You can explore more of her Weirdly Whimsical World and support her writing at patreon.com/Dorothy Tinker.

About the Designers

Cover Artist

Verstandt R. A. Shelton is Inklings Publishing's cover artist. Growing up as a childhood misfit, Verstandt R. A. Shelton wiled away the hours daydreaming of floating in space and sitting at the bottom of the ocean floor. A disquieting obsession for the less beaten paths of philosophical ponderings and environmental extremes led him to stumble into the murky depths of the writerly craft. You can find him today chained in the back of his closet with the lights out, a bottle of whiskey in hand, and the ghosts of his inspirations (Stephen King, Clive Barker, Milton, Lovecraft, and Dante) breathing down his neck, writing stories to terrify the world. His lovely wife, Jennifer, and his cat, Siouxsie Q, worry for his safety.

Copyediting and Formatting

Dorothy Tinker started D Tinker Editing with a love of language and a keen eye for details. As a published author herself, she understands the personal nature of any writer's work and strives to help each client's words and style shine. D Tinker Editing offers services such as developmental editing, copyediting, proofreading, and formatting. For more information or a price quote, please email dtinker@balanceofseven.com.

Other Great Reads

Come peruse the beasts within. This collection by Jae Mazer is filled with short stories and flash fiction that is gouged by talons, covered in feathers, slick with scales, coiled in tentacles, stripped of flesh, and even tainted by the beasts we call human. Find this and Jae Mazer's other titles at any book or ebook retailer.

Not sure what you're looking for? Pick up an anthology from the Eclectic Writings Series. Each is based on a theme and

features a variety of great authors. This collection is guaranteed to surprise and entertain.

The Twisted Reveries Series by Meg Hafdahl debuted in October 2015 with *Thirteen Tales of the Macabre*. In October 2016, *Tales from Willoughby* followed. Get your copy of these spine-tingling volumes today and enjoy short stories by this great female voice in horror!

Begin the tale of Willoughby in Meg Hafdahl's debut novel, *Her Dark Inheritance*. Follow Daphne as she uncovers the secrets her mother kept from her for all her life. Just how deeply into Willoughby's dark history do those secrets tie?

This epic fantasy novel, *Tarbin's True Heir*, is the first of Kelly Lynn Colby's The Recharging series. Follow a pair of royal twins as they go head-to-head to prove to all peoples which of them, older sister or younger brother, is the True Heir.

THE RECHARGING
BOOK ONE

TARBIN'S
TRUE
HEIR

KELLY LYNN COLBY

Kira has been given up by her parents as an infirm, to live out her days as a ward of the government. But how many days does she have? And is there a secret haven where her limited time might be extended? Get *Infirm*, and join Kira as she fights to live in this first installment of the Kira Chronicles.

When Genie and her friends make a wish at a local fountain, she thinks it's ridiculous, at worst. That is, until one of her friends, Beth, is kidnapped. Now Genie and the others must travel through a portal to Avalon—a land of magic, Knights of the Round Table, and the Lady of the Lake. Can the friends find their inner strength together, or will Beth, Avalon, and Earth be lost to evil?

The anthologies in the Perceptions Series are collections of short stories, poems, and nonfiction articles based on themes written for children grades three through six by a variety of authors. As with all Inklings Children Division books, each volume contains questions and activities for parents and educators to extend learning.

Perceptions Series
Volume One

Edited by: Fern Brady

The Smiley Face Blatoon, now available in a bilingual Spanish/English edition, launched Inklings Children Division in Summer 2015. First-place winner of the Texas Authors Association's Best Picture Book for All Ages, this, and all Inklings Children Division books, contains extensive activities, discussion questions, and cross-curricular work, as well as other tools for parents and educators.

In this second picture book by Lady Nefari Ydarb, meet Ella Peluchie, a black Labrador. She has to sit still for a photo shoot, but her doggie mind wanders to the large water bowl in Auntie's backyard. Will she be able to get through the process of having her portrait taken?

Picture Day, Ella!

Lady Nefari Ydarb

This international legal thriller is the first book in the Roberto Duran series. Get to know this intrepid criminal attorney from Houston as he fights to uncover the truth and save a young Mexican socialite from wrongful incarceration.

This bilingual resource provides insight into the workings of a civil lawsuit in terms anyone can understand. Great for interpreters, as well as authors who are writing legal thrillers.

Interpreters'
Anatomy *of a*
Civil Lawsuit

Anatomía *de un*
Juicio Civil *para*
Intérpretes Judiciales

Ramón M. del Villar

Attorney at Law
Federally Certified Court Interpreter
State Licensed Court Interpreter

Licenciado en Derecho
Intérprete Judicial Certificación Federal
Intérprete Judicial Texas, Maestría

Follow Inklings Publishing by:

Signing up for our newsletter at www.inklingspublishing.com

Liking our Facebook page

And following our tweets